MW01703691

Once Upon a Beast

Once Upon a Beast

A Bourbon Falls Romance

Kyra Jacobs

TULE
PUBLISHING

Once Upon a Beast

Copyright© 2023 Kyra Jacobs

Tule Publishing First Printing, August 2023

The Tule Publishing, Inc.

ALL RIGHTS RESERVED

First Publication by Tule Publishing 2023

Cover design by Carpe Librum Book Design

No part of this book may be used or reproduced in any manner whatsoever without written permission except in the case of brief quotations embodied in critical articles and reviews.

This is a work of fiction. Names, characters, places, and incidents are products of the author's imagination or are used fictitiously. Any resemblance to actual events, locales, organizations, or persons, living or dead, is entirely coincidental.

ISBN: 978-1-959988-70-0

Dedication

To Danielle, who's shown me just how beautiful bold women can be.

Chapter One

DELANEY BROOKS WAS closing up for the night when Bourbon Falls, Indiana, lost power. After five minutes of waiting with no improvement in sight, she scribbled instructions for her business partner to run their end-of-day reports before Oak Barrel Farms Landscaping reopened in the morning. Chase would understand. Besides, she was due to volunteer at Brooks Books in less than an hour. Though, if the town's electricity remained out all night, their family bookstore might have to close early as well.

As happy as she was to help there, a rare weeknight off wouldn't be so bad.

She taped her note for Chase to the inside of the front door and did one last scan of their shop: checkout counter was clean, wooden floors swept, indoor plants on display watered, knickknacks restocked and dusted. Some days, she had to pinch herself, the landscaping company she'd founded with longtime family friend Chase Redding still feeling like a dream come true. She made sure the light switches were all off to conserve electricity whenever it returned, then headed for the door.

It was common for summer storms to roll through northern Indiana, but losing power happened only during the big ones. Judging by the wind howling through the grove of oak trees surrounding her shop, tonight's was shaping up to be a doozie. She hurried out to her vehicle, grateful for the thick canopy of leaves overhead, and prayed her friends and family were already home and safe from the storm.

Del turned out onto the road leading back into town, rain pelting her windshield faster than her wipers could keep up. Just as she began to wonder if it might be best to turn back, a bolt of lightning struck a tree up ahead, sending an explosion of sparks into the air. Del slammed on her brakes as the tree's charred remains toppled into the road; she skidded to a stop just shy of the landing zone.

Wow, that was close.

Heart pounding, she scanned the mess of limbs now scattered across the road—a mess that would need to be removed before someone came along and plowed into it. That's when she noticed the set of headlights approaching from the other direction. Del blared her horn, hoping to alert the other driver before they slammed into the downed tree and then into her. Fortunately, it worked.

Unfortunately, the other vehicle was much smaller and lighter than hers. Brakes locked, it hit a low spot in the road and hydroplaned across a patch of standing water. A streak of white veered off the road, tore through the adjoining yard, and buried itself in the jumble of weeds and long-forgotten shrubs that served as the entryway to their town's newest and most reclusive resident:

Isaac Manning, aka Harry the Hermit.

Del threw her truck into park and jumped out to drag the debris as best she could to the side of the road. The driving rain did her no favors, quickly soaking her to the bone. Road hazard cleared, she turned her attention to the other vehicle, which had yet to move from its jungle destination. She hurried toward it, casting a quick glance toward the nearby driveway.

So far, no Harry. Thank goodness for small miracles.

Oh, they'd wanted to think the best of the newcomer. Had even tried to think of logical reasons for why he'd ignore repeated attempts to deliver home-baked cookies by Bourbon Falls' Welcome Wagon. But when he'd come flying out of his garage, headed straight for a Cub Scout troop selling popcorn that second week—wild-eyed, shrieking, and waving a broom over his head—the troop hightailed it out of there. After that, the town collectively rolled up its welcome mat and let the man be. Thankfully, no one had seen hide nor hair of him since.

Del made a beeline past his drive toward the stranded car, not wanting to break the town's lucky streak. Overgrown landscaping awaited her on its opposite side, a sea of thistles as tall as her vying for space among neglected Knock Out roses. She wove through the mess as best she could, water squishing between her toes every step of the way.

Definitely gonna need to stop at home to change before heading to the bookstore now. She knew no one would complain if stopping home for dry clothes caused her to be a few minutes late. Her aunt Faye owned the store and was always grateful for help, no matter how large or small.

In years past, business at the bookstore was booming and they employed an evening staff. But that was before a big book box store opened in neighboring Warsaw. Now it was up to the family to pitch in if they wanted their mother's legacy to live on.

Thankfully, so far, everyone still did.

Worries about the bookstore came to a grinding halt as Del drew close enough to recognize the vehicle protruding from the township's shaggiest arborvitae: a white Pontiac Vibe, her sixteen-year-old niece's car.

"Brooklyn?" She moved faster now, thistles and bramble tearing at her exposed skin. "Brooklyn, is that you?"

"Aunt Del?" Oh, lord, it was her. What on earth had she been doing driving in the middle of a storm?

"Yes! Are you hurt?"

"I don't think so."

Relief washed over her as she ran. "Okay, hang on, I'm almost to you."

"Hang on?" Brooklyn asked. "I'm totally stuck—where could I possibly go?"

Ah, teenage sarcasm. Del took it as a good sign and continued through the vegetation.

"Stop!"

Oh no.

Del slid to a halt at the unexpected deep voice, on the lookout for a crazy broom-wielding man. "Hello?" she called, squinting into the pouring rain. "Is someone there?"

"Yes. And you're on private property."

She turned in the direction of the voice, but still saw no one. Maybe Harry wasn't ready to come out from hiding yet. Fine by her. "Listen, I'm Delaney Brooks, and my niece—"

"Is also trespassing. Now leave, before I call the police."

Her gaze swiveled from the voice to Brooklyn's location. "Buddy, do you not see the car wedged into your landscaping?"

"The what?"

Del was about to tell Mr. Unwelcoming just what she thought of his threat when her gaze landed on a small black box mounted to Harry's mailbox. He had a security camera now?

On a growl, Del started forward once more, needing to get to Brooklyn to make sure she was all right. Their ridiculous town hermit could go ahead and call the cops for all she cared. At least Earl would be man enough to come out into the elements and help them.

Then again, maybe that wouldn't be such a good idea. Who knew what something like this could do to Brooklyn's driving record.

"Is anyone hurt?" Harry called. "Do you need me to call

an ambulance?"

Okay, maybe the guy wasn't a complete jerk. "I don't know yet!"

Another fifteen steps or so and she reached Brooklyn's car. The driver's side window was down, the car's interior lit by the glow of a cell phone screen. Del squirmed her way through broken branches to get to her niece and was relieved to find the view devoid of blood.

"Honey, are you sure you're not hurt?"

Brooklyn lowered her phone in midtext. "I'm fine, but that was Harry, wasn't it? What if he goes all crazy on us? Or calls the police? Will they take me to juvie? Or take away my car? Aunt Del, I just got this car. I don't want to have to go back to walking to school!"

"Whoa, slow down there, sweetheart. Everything is going to be all right. What's important is that you're not hurt."

"But Mom will—"

"We'll worry about your mom and Harry later, okay? First, deep breaths. We can't think if we're too busy panicking."

Brooklyn frowned and took a slightly longer breath. "Fine, now what?"

"Let's have you put the car in reverse and see if we can't get you backed out of this mess."

"I tried that before you got here. The tires spin, but the car doesn't budge."

Del sighed. Of course this wasn't going to be easy.

"You must be stuck on something, let me check. Wait—when did you crack your phone screen?"

"Um"—Brooklyn tucked her phone under one leg—"before…"

"Brooklyn Annette French, do *not* tell me you were texting and driving."

"When?"

"*Brooklyn.*"

"What? The weather alarm went off and I tried to silence it."

Del shot her a "don't BS me" look. "We'll talk about this later. Right now, we need to get you out of Harry's yard and back on the road. Where were you even going in the middle of this storm, anyway?"

"To the farm. I wanted to make sure the ducklings were okay."

Del pinched the bridge of her nose. "Next time it's storming? You call Grandpa and let him give you a phone update instead, okay?"

At Brooklyn's sullen nod, Delaney ducked under the nearest mangled branch and shimmied her way toward the front bumper. Though she didn't have a clear view, there didn't seem to be anything preventing the car from backing up. More likely, the rain-soaked grass wasn't providing enough traction for the Vibe to escape its evergreen jail.

"I think our best bet is to try to pull you out," Del said. "Sit tight, I'll be right back."

She eased out of the arborvitae and spun to find a man she didn't recognize exiting a late model SUV, now parked on Manning's driveway. Surely, that couldn't be Harry; hermits couldn't look that appealing. This guy was tall, dark, and handsome…and now soaked to the bone like her. His black V-neck tee and khaki cargo shorts showed off lean limbs and sun-kissed skin. A Yankees ballcap was tugged low over shoulder-length dark hair that curled around his ears, and scruffy facial hair covered his face and neck.

Nope, definitely not someone from around here, she decided as he approached. But who was he? Beneath the cap's brim, dark eyes were fixed intently on her.

"Well?" he demanded.

ISAAC MANNING STOPPED a short distance from the woman he'd seen on his surveillance footage. He was afraid to get closer, but he also needed to know that everyone was okay. Delaney had on a logo polo shirt and jean capris, both now covered in mud and burrs. Short, cropped hair was plastered to her head, which drew his attention to the bright-blue eyes assessing him. He prayed his hat and unshaven face were disguise enough to keep her from recognizing him.

After all, he hadn't moved halfway across the country and stayed hidden for the past six months to blow it in his first interaction with someone from Bourbon Falls.

Well, first *real* interaction. That carload of Boy Scouts hadn't stuck around long enough for him to explain that a bat had just tried to dive-bomb him in his garage. He could only guess the rumors that exchange had caused. Even so, he couldn't sit inside and do nothing, knowing someone had driven into his yard and could possibly be injured.

Though it'd been pouring when he first exited his vehicle, the rain now slowed to an annoying drizzle. In the improved visibility he could see that, sure enough, a little white sedan was half buried in one of the evergreen behemoths that stood sentry to his rental's driveway. He looked from the set of glowing taillights to Delaney and tipped his chin toward the car.

"Your niece—is she hurt?"

The tension in her shoulders eased. "Thankfully, no. At least, she insists she isn't."

"I'm glad to hear it."

Truly, he'd hate for anyone to be hurt. Would hate even more having police and EMS staff arriving and wanting to speak with him. The fewer visitors, the better.

"Yes, a huge relief for sure. Unfortunately, her car's wedged in there pretty good. It's gonna take some extra muscle to get her out."

No surprise there, considering how far into the shrub her car now sat. His gaze shifted from the vehicle to the messy trail stretched out behind it. He had no idea how fast she'd been going, but those deep tire ruts seemed to run a country mile. On the bright side, her path of destruction had also mowed over a good chunk of the thistles on this side of his entryway.

Man, had he known how effective a slide off could be with clearing weeds, Isaac might have tried this himself a few weeks back. Landscaping hadn't been a priority of his since relocating here. Which, as he stood here now taking it all in, was clearly evident. Would his renter's insurance cover all of this?

"You didn't happen to bring a tow strap along, did you?" Delaney asked.

"A tow…strap?" Surely, she had to be kidding.

"No worries."

She started for a huge silver pickup parked by the road, where he assumed she had left her cell phone. But instead of a phone, Delaney started back with, sure enough, a worn, yellow tow strap.

"Shouldn't we just call a tow truck?" he asked.

She snorted. "Oh, ye of little faith."

He watched her pass, debating whether or not to insist they call someone; he had zero experience with this sort of thing. Then again, if she knew what she was doing, it would minimize the number of visitors he had tonight. Already, two was more than he was comfortable with.

"All right, Brooklyn," she said. "Keep it in park until I say otherwise. Got it?"

"Okay, Aunt Del."

Isaac hurried to join them, not wishing to wound Del's ego further but also not wanting to look like an indifferent jerk. Without pause, she crawled under the backend of Brooklyn's car to affix the first end of the strap. As she eased out from under it, Isaac reached to help her up. For a moment, she just stared at his outstretched hand. Had he accidentally offended her a second time?

Just as he began to think she wouldn't accept the assist, she clasped his hand like they were about to arm wrestle and tried pulling herself up to a standing position. But the grass beneath them was slippery from the rain, and what started as a smooth move ended with her tumbling into his chest.

"Sorry," Del mumbled, her cheeks flushed.

"No worries," he mumbled back, holding on until he knew she'd found her footing. "It's pretty slick out."

She stalked off on a nod, unraveling the tow strap as she went.

It's pretty slick out? He dragged a hand down the side of his face. *That's the best I could do?*

Not that it really mattered if he sounded lame. Isaac wasn't here to make friends or grow roots in the community—he was only here until it was safe to move back home. He caught up with her a moment later, taking the tow strap when offered. Then she climbed into the pickup and made a smooth three-point turn, positioning her truck on the side of the road. Nope, definitely not her first rodeo.

"What am I going to tell you to do when I give the signal, B?" she called to Brooklyn as she left the truck to collect the tow strap from Isaac.

"Um…put it in neutral?"

"That's my girl." Del gave him a nod. "See? We'll have her out of there in no time."

"Great."

After all, the sooner they were gone, the sooner he could relax. Then it could get back to being just him and his rescue dog Louie up at the house, hiding away from the world. For how much longer, he didn't know.

Lightning flashed in the distance, followed by a rumble of thunder louder than the last one. Round two of tonight's storm seemed to be rolling in. Hopefully, they'd be done with all of this before it arrived.

As Del attached the tow strap to her truck and double-checked the work, Isaac rubbed his palm, wishing it would stop tingling after taking her hand. Had it been a spark of attraction, or was it because he hadn't had physical contact with another person in months? Whatever the reason, it wasn't enough to shake him off his goals. Neither were those long legs, perfect butt—yes, he'd watched as she'd climbed in and out of that behemoth truck—and ocean-blue eyes. He was here to lie low while the dumpster fire out east ran out of fuel, nothing more.

"Ready, Brooklyn?"

"Um…ready?"

Isaac grinned at the contrast between Del's confident

voice and her niece's nervous one. For the briefest of moments, it brought back fond memories of childhood and time spent with his favorite uncle. He glanced toward the house. Frank would have loved this place. That project junkie would have called it a gem in the rough and volunteered to help make it shine again, even if it was just a rental.

His gaze shifted once more to the yard, grimacing again at the long stretch of ruts that ran from Brooklyn's car to the road. They were fixable enough, but the huge tree/bush thing that had half swallowed the sedan looked done for, which meant calling someone out to cut it down before it fell and blocked his drive. Or worse, fell on him or someone else.

Maybe he should call Will in the morning and see what he wanted done with the yard. It was his rental, after all. Though, Isaac would need to skim over the part about interacting with Delaney and her niece. No sense in making Will all paranoid again. He'd flipped out enough after learning of Isaac's weekly late-night grocery runs in the next town over—something he refused to give up.

Del's truck inched forward, and the tow strap slowly went taut. It felt weird, being a bystander to it all, but the look of concentration in Del's reflection told him she'd done this before. Her engine revved steadily louder until the little Pontiac was tugged free from the evergreen mess, limbs creaking and snapping around it as the car slowly made its escape. Relief shone on Brooklyn's face after the truck pulled her car off his lawn and back onto the road. Brooklyn's cheeks reddened as he approached to make sure she was truly all right.

"I am *so* sorry about your yard. And the big bush thing." She got out of her car to get a better look. "Maybe we can straighten it with some stakes in the ground or something?"

"And then what?" Del called, untethering their vehicles. "Wait for the next storm to blow it over?"

She approached and pulled her niece into a tight hug, silencing any retort from the teen. Brooklyn hugged her back, the two clearly very close. Now that he could see her better, aside from the longer hair and abundance of freckles, and her being far drier than the rest of them, the family resemblance between Brooklyn and her aunt was striking.

A bright bolt of lightning forked in the not-so-far distance, its booming thunderclap reminding them the night's storms weren't quite done.

"Sorry, kiddo, but stakes aren't going to fix this. That arborvitae needs to come down before it falls on anyone. Plus, you've got some major ruts to fill in for Mr. Manning."

Funny, he didn't remember telling her his name. "Please, just call me Isaac. And don't worry about the ruts. I'll take care of all this."

Well, hopefully his insurance company would be taking care of it all. He'd find out soon enough. Del, however, frowned.

"Absolutely not. Brooklyn made a mess of this place, and Brooklyn's gonna help—"

Guitar strumming interrupted her, and Del pulled a cell phone from her back pocket.

"Sorry, Faye, I'm running a bit late. I'll—*what*?" She grimaced. "Okay, we'll be right there."

Del disconnected and met his gaze. "I'm afraid we're going to need to work out the details another time. Our bookstore's roof just sprang a leak."

Had she just said their…bookstore?

Brooklyn's eyes widened. "It didn't."

"It did." She hitched a thumb to their vehicles. "The ducklings will have to wait. You're coming with me."

Isaac felt a swell of relief. They were leaving. "That's fine, you two go handle the roof thing and I'll just call my insurance company tomor—"

"No!" the girls cried in unison.

Del stepped closer, a pleading look in her bright-blue eyes. "Please don't call this in. If insurance gets involved, things might get messy for Brooklyn. And expensive." She ran a hand over her wet hair. "Look, I can cut the arborvitae down on my lunch hour tomorrow. Okay?"

"But what about the rest of my yard?"

"I promise, we'll make it right. Just…give us a little time."

As much as he hated to think how much attention his mess of a yard would attract, Isaac hated the idea of having to deal with insurance adjusters or worried business partners far more. Hopefully, this Delaney woman would be good to her word. He'd give her a day, no more. After that, he made no promises.

"Fine. You've got until tomorrow evening. And good luck with the leak."

Chapter Two

DEL LEANED AGAINST the checkout counter at Brooks Books, trying to finally catch her breath. Between unshelving hundreds of books and making several trips to and from the hardware store next door gathering five-gallon buckets for catching rainwater and oscillating fans to help dry the place, she was nearly spent. Thankfully, the buckets seemed to be working, and today's rainclouds had finally moved east, which meant they were out of danger. For now, anyway.

"Is this the first time the roof has leaked?"

"No." Aunt Faye sat atop her favorite stool on the opposite side of the counter, looking as exhausted as Del felt. "I'm thinking your mother had issues when she and your father first rented this space. At the time, someone on the town council owned his own roofing company and volunteered to patch it. But he'd warned council that they should be putting money away to replace the roof in the next five years. Twenty-some years later, we're still waiting for that new roof."

Del shook her head. She'd attended more town council

meetings than she could shake a stick at, and the resounding theme was always the same: when it came to large capital projects, there simply wasn't enough money to go around. But surely they would step in and do something now. The town owned this building, renting half its space to her family for their bookstore and the other half to George Haines. Haines Hardware and Brooks Books had become staples in this town, places everyone came to visit. She doubted either operated much in the black, but in small towns it wasn't just about the money—places like these brought the community together. Why, she couldn't even imagine Bourbon Falls without these two landmarks.

Her gaze swept through their beloved store. She'd grown up within these beautiful brick walls, three-quarters of which held shelves lined with books of every shape and size. Had played hide-and-seek countless times with her sisters among the shorter, two-sided free-standing shelves that wove through the middle of the space and gone sliding in her socks across its waxed hardwood floors as often as they'd been able to get away with it.

Tonight, however, her heart ached at the sight. Its western wall stood half bare, the books they'd been able to salvage from its collection relocated to tables in the back room while the small number lost to water damage lay in a sad pile at its base. A small collection of fans was also aimed in that direction, aiding in the drying process. Atop many of the free-standing interior shelves were a smattering of buckets, placed strategically to collect rainwater that earlier had been streaming in from the aged roof. And the wooden floors, notoriously spotless and shined to perfection, lay dirtied with footprints and water-soaked towels.

They were all lucky Faye had been here when the leaks began. If this had happened overnight or on a Sunday when the store was closed, the losses would have been far more severe.

"Then we'll have to petition that they finally step up and make these repairs, before you or George loses any more inventory," Del said.

"Did it hit his side of the building pretty hard, too?" Faye asked.

"No, but he was watching just in case a leak sprang up over there. Hopefully, the town will send someone out here tomorrow to get up on the roof and at least patch what they can. Then you can get your store back in order, and he won't have to worry about the issue spreading to his side."

"I hope so. Goodness knows I won't be getting much sleep until I know we're out of the woods. Speaking of which," Faye said with raised brow. "Why do you look like you spent the afternoon playing *in* the woods?"

Del looked from her muddied and burr-speckled attire to her niece, who was stepping through the front door after dumping another water-filled bucket. "Why don't you ask Brooklyn?"

"Ask me what?" she asked, dropping into a nearby folding chair. It seemed even the youngest of the Brooks girls was worn out from tonight's activities.

"Why your aunt looks like she spent the afternoon mudwrestling in the woods."

"It was the stupid tree's fault, okay? If it hadn't fallen across the road, I wouldn't have slid into that big bush."

Faye's hand flew to her chest. "You went off the road? Oh dear heavens. I take it you're okay?"

"Yeah, but now I have a dent in my front bumper." Brooklyn dropped her face into her hands. "Mom's probably gonna ground me for a year."

"Accidents happen, Little B, she knows that," Del said. "Though, if we can keep Isaac from filing a claim with his insurance, that'd probably help keep your mom a little happier. I'd hate to see what an accident would do to your rates."

"Or we could just not tell her at all and I could make something up about the dent," Brooklyn said in a sing-song voice.

Ha, like that was going to happen.

"Time-out," Faye said. "You haven't told Mia about this yet? And who is Isaac?"

Del pushed off from the counter, hands in her hair. "Oh my gosh—with everything going on here, I forgot to call her!"

Her oldest sister was going to let her have it for sure, especially since Brooklyn had just spent the last three days staying with her while Mia was at a teacher's conference in Illinois. What kind of responsible aunt forgot to notify her sister of a freaking car accident? She started pacing the checkout area. Surely, there was a way to bring it up belatedly without her sister going ballistic.

"I think you should keep forgetting. Also, Isaac is the hermit that lives next to Grandpa," Brooklyn said, interrupting her fretting.

Aunt Faye gasped. "This all happened in Isaac Manning's yard?"

Yes, Isaac Manning was a household name in Bourbon Falls. Not because he'd ever come into town and introduced himself, but because the woman who ran the town's mail route tipped them off. The broom fiasco had put her in the center of attention for at least a week.

"Yes," Del said, still pacing. "But there were no brooms involved this time. In fact, once he realized Brooklyn was stuck in his overgrown mess of landscaping, he stopped trying to scare us away and actually came outside to help."

"Really?" Faye asked.

"Yep. And Aunt Del thinks he's totally hot, too."

Del came to an abrupt halt. "When did I say that?"

"See?" Brooklyn smirked. "She's getting all red."

Faye arched a knowing brow; Del wished she had a book handy to hide behind.

"So what if he was easy on the eyes? Lots of guys around here are like that."

Which wasn't exactly true. Being a small town, Bourbon Falls didn't have lots of guys—hot or otherwise—and definitely not a surplus of them in her age group. It also had zero men with the same caliber of Isaac's handsomeness, an opinion she dared not mention at this moment.

Because yes, even drenched, the man had looked mighty fine.

But what she'd been drawn to even more was his concern for Brooklyn. He didn't have to come down from his house in the pouring rain, but he had. Plus, he'd agreed not to call the cops or his insurance agent—also things he hadn't had to do. And he'd shown up sans broom, which was another surprise. Maybe the town hermit wasn't so bad after all.

Brooklyn clasped her hands and put them under her chin, eyelashes batting. "Oh, Isaac. *Please* don't call your insurance company. I'd *love* to come back and clean this all up with you."

"Really?" Del planted a hand on each hip. "I save your butt by pulling you out of the mud and keeping him from reporting the accident, and this is the thanks I get?"

Faye covered her mouth, trying to hide a grin and failing miserably. She looked to Brooklyn and said, "He must have been quite a looker."

"I guess so. I mean, if you're into old guys and stuff."

"Old guys? He can't be much older than me!" Del pinched the bridge of her nose. Getting defensive would only make her niece's accusation that much more believable.

And so what if the guy was good-looking? It didn't mean she was going to ask him out on a date or anything. Heck, the guy never left his house! Besides, dates led to relationships, and goodness knew she was done with those for a while. Maybe for forever, as badly as she'd been burned the last go around.

Having a little fun here and there? Sure.

Getting serious with anyone? Wasn't gonna happen.

Nope, no dating in her future, just her holding up her end of the bargain by putting the guy's yard back in order. Then she could go on her way, and he could go back to doing whatever handsome hermits did all day. Oh, and she needed to tell Mia belatedly about her daughter's fender bender without being disowned.

"Maybe instead of you two making fun of me, you could do something a little more productive—like help me think of what to tell your mother."

"Tell me what?"

The trio spun in unison. With all the fans going, no one had heard Mia Brooks-French arrive. She stepped out from the back hall, a wary look on her face.

Del forced the most angelic smile she could muster. "Uh, hiya, Sis."

ISAAC DRAGGED HIMSELF out of bed early the next morning

in advance of a scheduled video conference call. There were perks to working from home these past several months, one of which was not having to take the early subway train to get to the office on time. Then again, he was generally there an hour before everyone else, so "late" was really only ever by his standards; his partner William McManus and the rest of their team usually rolled in somewhere between eight and nine.

Life in the Big Apple was all hustle and bustle.

Life here in Indiana was mind-numbingly dull.

Showered and dressed—professionally as far as they knew, a long-sleeved button-down and tie from the waist up, jogging shorts and white socks from the waist down—he grabbed a cup of coffee and dropped into a seat before his laptop camera. When he'd first moved to Indiana, he'd looked forward to these calls because he missed his colleagues. Over time, however, he'd begun to dread them. Anymore, the incoming bad news outweighed the good. It seemed for every new project won, two existing ones had been lost.

Isaac leaned back and stared at his rental's faded popcorn ceiling. He'd hoped his decision to move west and diminish his presence at Manning & McManus IT Solutions would have spared the company from taking the brunt of last summer's social media disaster. Unfortunately, the fire had grown too big, too fast to be extinguished by such a simple move. Now their once-thriving app development company, focused on helping upstarts and small businesses build the websites and sales tools they needed to grow, was struggling to stay afloat.

Today's meeting was to review current projects and any other potential leads they might have a chance at winning. Because if there was a chance, M&M needed to submit a bid. Yes, proposals took time, but with their current lull in work, time was something they had plenty of.

Money, however, was not.

Their budget had been slashed to the bone in every area but payroll, thanks to the added expense of PR damage control. If things didn't start to turn around soon, they'd need to consider layoffs. But who could they possibly choose to hand a pink slip? Each member of their team was like family to them.

Isaac prayed it wouldn't come to that. If only they could convince their clients—both existing and prospective—to move past the misunderstanding that'd spiraled out of their control. Or, better yet, find a way to extinguish the fire out east without any further harm to their company.

Isaac logged into the web call, his name still appearing as Robert on the screen, then pulled out the agenda he'd drafted. For years he'd second-guessed Will's suggestion to use his middle name since Robert sounded more established and businesslike than Isaac. After the mess he'd found himself in last fall, though, it'd turned out to be a godsend. "Robert" could be on hiatus while Isaac could quietly help keep their company moving forward. Though their team now knew the two names were one and the same person, they continued to address him as Robert for simplicity's sake.

Soon their faces began to appear one by one in little boxes on his screen. Sam, Vivvy, AJ, and Monique—their development team, composed of once-fledgling programmers who'd shown promise and initiative. To date, he'd not been wrong about a single one. Up next popped Ashley and Carmen, Will's administrative team members whom they'd all be lost without.

Man, he missed everyone. Missed being able to pop into their cubicles and assist with coding struggles. Missed watching Ashley get everyone's coffee orders wrong. Missed just shooting the breeze with his team about a ballgame they'd seen the night before.

Which was why he had to find a way to fix this mess he'd caused. If hiding out in the rental that used to belong to Will's great aunt wasn't helping their business, then it was time to try a new approach. Hopefully, the team would be on board with his ideas.

As the others engaged in their usual office banter, Isaac's mind drifted to the prior night and a certain blue-eyed beauty who'd paid him a surprise visit. Was that the reason he was battling loneliness today? Because he'd had a taste of human interaction and was now craving more?

The image of Del climbing in and out of that huge pickup truck, looking as though she'd done it a million times, came back to him. Something told him she'd do that a million more, too. The woman wore confidence like a second skin—something he used to do in his line of work as well. Used to, before the whole Katrina Gibbons incident.

"Good to see you this morning, Robert. How's life treating you in Cornville?"

Isaac grinned at Carmen's teasing. She'd grown up in an Indiana farming town not far from here; thus, he knew better than to correct her. "Boring as ever," he answered.

She chuckled. "And Louie?"

"Asleep on my feet."

"Excellent. Well, it looks like we're just waiting on Will to join the call," she said. "We'll give him a few more minutes before I send out the 'hurry up already' text."

Her head shake elicited a round of soft laughter, and Isaac's melancholy grew. For the umpteenth time, he kicked himself for not listening to his gut when their mail courier had first asked him out for coffee. He'd tried to be the nice guy, and coffee sounded harmless enough. He just never could have guessed how wrong that assumption had been.

Well, technically, the coffee had been harmless. The woman, not so much.

"Louie, buddy, I can't feel my toes."

He gently slid his feet out from under the rump of his stocky English bulldog and reached to give Louie a scratch behind the ears. They said man's best friend was his dog, something Isaac hadn't fully comprehended until rescuing his deaf pooch from the pound two years ago. Louie's former owners claimed they didn't have the time or patience to deal with a dog who wouldn't listen.

Morons. If they'd taken him to a single vet trip, they would have found out why. But their loss was Isaac's gain, and he'd done all he could to make sure Louie was living his best life. They'd even come up with a language all their own, using hand signs and other visual cues. Judging by the way Louie's whole body wiggled with happiness at his every touch, the dog knew how much he was loved and appreciated.

Touch.

Isaac grinned at the memory of Del falling into him the night before as he'd helped her from the ground, and how they'd both behaved like awkward teenagers afterward. Clearly, he was out of practice "peopling." While that might have explained his reaction to the accidental collision, hers was a bit of a mystery; Del didn't come across as a woman who embarrassed easily.

Maybe she was shier than she'd portrayed.

Maybe she had a boyfriend.

Maybe he should stop thinking about her, because it did him no good to dwell on a chance interaction with someone he didn't plan to live near for long.

His gaze shifted to the rental insurance policy he'd dug out the night before, in case she didn't show today. The lonely side of his heart hoped she'd hold to her promise; the smarter side hoped she wouldn't. Then again, her returning to take down that damaged evergreen would cost him less, so that meant his smarter side was rooting for her to show, too.

Isaac blew out a sigh. Why did life always have to be so complicated?

Will's ever-booming voice broke through his reverie as another familiar face appeared on Isaac's computer screen. "Gooooood morning, everyone. How's Team M&M doing today?"

Lively chatter ensued, and Isaac refocused on the task at hand. This company, this team, was what he was most passionate about. The relocation and loneliness were temporary, a means to an end. Will had promised to do all he could to douse the dumpster fire. Until then, Isaac had to be patient.

Someone on the call mentioned a great book they'd been reading. Had Delaney's group been able to save their bookstore? In the past, he wouldn't have hesitated to go help a family in need. But for the first time he could remember, fear had held him back. For that, he felt like a coward.

It wasn't fair, the way public perception had eclipsed his world. But then, no one ever said life would be.

Patience. A sleepy Louie settled onto his feet once more. *This will all blow over in time. Enjoy the big-city break so you can go back recharged.*

That's exactly how he would return to the scene. Recharged, and with an abundance of newly gained perspective.

How better to understand their customers' needs for working remotely than experiencing it for himself?

He glanced from his computer desk, sitting in what was supposed to be a formal dining room, to the living room that held nothing but a television, a single recliner, and side table. Isaac hoped his customers were living more exciting lives than this.

Across the space, sunshine streamed in through the front windows. Hopefully, the morning sun would dry the yard out before he and Louie's midmorning walk. Because the way he was feeling now—missing his friends, missing his hometown—he was going to need some fresh air after this call. Something to clear his mind of the past, so he could capitalize on all the possibilities waiting for him in the future.

A future that most definitely did not involve small towns in Indiana with wrecked landscaping or beautiful, overconfident, truck-driving women.

Chapter Three

DEL BOLTED UPRIGHT when her alarm sounded the next morning, heart pounding and covers askew. She'd been dreaming, chased through town hall by a giant, talking chainsaw. Isaac had appeared in one of the doorways she was rushing past, waving a broom at her while yelling to stay off his lawn. Awake and grateful to have been rescued from the nonsense, she silenced her alarm.

Hopefully, that hadn't been a premonition of how he would greet her today.

On a yawn, she rolled out of bed, pushed the hermit from her mind, and started getting ready for work. Nine was later than she usually went in, but thankfully Chase had agreed to swap his closing duties for her opening ones. A real blessing, since she'd stayed to help Faye with the bookstore until nearly dawn. She prayed the tarps they'd put on the roof last night had held.

Del checked her phone before showering. No texts yet from Faye—was it too soon to start worrying? Or was it that no news was good news? Surely, their town would rally around the old building and do all it could to preserve a vital piece of its history.

Dressed and refreshed but in need of caffeine, she headed to the kitchen—one of her favorite rooms in the Craftsman home, so welcoming and sunny. It'd been a sad little bungalow when she'd first toured it, its former owners unable to keep up with the aging property's maintenance. But she'd seen its potential, knew it still had great bones. And the best part was its location—just a short drive from her father's farm, and a backyard catty-corner to that of her oldest sister's slightly larger Craftsman.

Talk about hitting the real estate jackpot.

Aside from it needing considerable updating, anyway. She hadn't known much about home renovation back then, but worked with a lot of people who grew up in the skilled trades field. Thankfully, they were happy to trade their skills and knowledge for cold beer and cookouts.

That was one of the things she loved most about her hometown: its generosity. Recruiting volunteers wasn't something that required arm-twisting in Bourbon Falls. Rather, everyone rolled up their sleeves and tackled projects right alongside you. Well, except for maybe grouchy hermits.

Lucky for her, she didn't need help taking down that overgrown shrub.

Del made for her truck, mental wheels now turning with the day's tasks ahead. Soon she was headed down West Center Street, trading Bourbon Falls' cozy suburban yards for a seemingly endless sea of yellowing soybeans. A few miles more, she turned south on Elm Road and Brooklyn's ruts came into view, along with the semi-mangled evergreen mammoth she'd clobbered. Isaac had done nothing with any of it since they'd left last night, which was no surprise considering the condition of the rest of his landscaping.

Really, though, it wasn't her place to judge. If he wanted to avoid yardwork, that was his choice. She did her thing, and everyone else could do theirs. If he was a mega introvert or just someone who grew up hating people, she wasn't going to try to talk him out of it.

She was a landscaper, not a shrink.

A good thing, too—that yard was going to need a lot of work. Hopefully, she could knock out the restorations in a day or two. Goodness knew Faye would need help getting the bookstore put back together.

Another quarter mile down Elm, and her beloved Oak Barrel Farms came into view. The former, easternmost acre of her father's farm had been cleared of all but the small island of oak trees surrounding a decades-old hunting cabin, which had since become OBF's storefront. A greenhouse had been erected behind the grove of oaks, and beyond that stood stockpiles of various stones and mulches.

Del turned off the main road and onto their business's shaded drive, on the lookout for any storm damage they might have sustained last night. Thankfully, everything looked as she remembered. Her father's dog Rex barked a hello from the shop's front porch as he did when her father was busy at the fire station—which was often, considering he was Bourbon Falls' long-time fire chief. Though the aging lab still had plenty of spunk in him, most days Rex followed her inside and spent the morning napping beneath their checkout counter.

After she'd given him a treat or two, of course. Good dogs always deserved treats.

Beyond Rex, Del spied a shaggy-haired blond through the office's screened door, a clipboard in one hand and coffee mug in his other. Though Chase Redding looked more surfer than landscaper, she wouldn't trade her partner-in-crime for the world. Like her father, Chase was a local fireman, which meant he worked a twenty-four hours on, forty-eight hours off rotation at the station. During his off times, he worked at Oak Barrel Farms handling the heavy lifting and coordinating delivery and planting crews.

Their partnership had gelled seamlessly from the start, which surprised no one—Chase was as close to a little brother as Del had ever known. Growing up, he'd spent more time at their place than his, partly because his home life sucked and partly because he'd been in love with Del's little sister since the first grade. Hopefully, one day Hannah would return home and mend the poor guy's broken heart.

Heck, mend all their hearts. It just wasn't the same in Bourbon Falls without her.

Del parked around back in one of their two executive parking spaces—a joke between her and Chase; both were nothing more than gravel rectangles wedged between scraggly trees—and stepped from her truck. The air beneath the oak canopy remained cool, though today was projected to be a scorcher. She drew in a deep breath, letting the earthy scents ground her before getting caught up in her day, then headed inside. Chase greeted her with a smile.

"Morning, sunshine."

"Good morning. Thanks again for opening for me today. I really needed that extra sleep."

"Not a problem. How's the bookstore?"

She grimaced, making her way through their cozy little showroom. Like her family had done with the bookstore's historic building, Del and Chase had preserved as much of the rustic feel of the cabin as they could. Some things they couldn't avoid changing, however, like adding indoor plumbing and heating and cooling units. But their custom-made display tables matched the log cabin vibes, and the neat and tidy potted domestic greenery for sale atop each brought a little bit of the outdoors in. It was a stark comparison to the disorganized mess she'd left in the wee hours of the morning.

"Still standing, so that's a good thing. You should have seen it, Chase. The roof's northeast corner was leaking like a sieve. We lost a few dozen books that didn't get moved fast enough, but most were in the used section. Sucks to lose any, though."

"Agreed. How's Faye taking it?"

"Oh, you know my aunt," Del said, putting her keys away with a grin. "Always looking at the bright side of things. She kept insisting it could have been a whole lot worse."

When she and Brooklyn weren't teasing me about Isaac, anyway. Which reminds me…

"Hey, any chance I can borrow one of the chainsaws over my lunch break? I offered to help with some storm damage cleanup."

Chase looked at her like she'd grown a third arm. "You know there are easier ways to take down bookshelves than with a chainsaw, right?"

"Not at the bookstore, you goof!" Del shook her head and laughed. "No, I'm helping a…friend with some downed branches and stuff."

"Well, that makes more sense. Yeah, no prob. Might need it this afternoon, though. Think you can have it back by maybe one o'clock? Or I could just meet you over there. I'm sure we could knock it out pretty quick if we tag-teamed it."

"No!"

Chase's brows rose in unison.

Oh, man, why on earth had her answer come out sounding so panicked? It wasn't like he would go and report Brooklyn to anyone if he found out why Del had cleanup work ahead of her today. Or did it maybe have more to do with *who* she was doing the work for?

Isaac in his drenched attire had put that long, lean body nicely on display. Would he look as delicious today in drier clothes? She felt her cheeks warm, which wouldn't help her end this conversation any sooner. Del faked a coughing fit, then grabbed her travel mug and took a long drink.

"Sorry, had a tickle in my throat."

"Uh-huh," Chase said with a wary eye. "Probably from all the dust that got kicked up moving books last night."

"Exactly." She took another long swig to emphasize her point. Though something told her he wasn't buying it. "Anyway, there isn't that much to clean up, so you don't need to waste your lunch break helping me on mine. Besides, someone's gotta stay here to man the store, right?"

Chase looked around their shop, currently empty of customers. Weekday foot traffic was minimal at best this late in the season. Which they both knew.

"Riiiight. Well, I'm gonna head out back and start loading the trailer for that Manchester job. But don't worry, I won't leave until you're back from running your errand. Wouldn't want us to miss any sales, you know."

He was goading her now, but Del wasn't biting. She didn't ask him about his personal life, so he didn't need to know about hers.

Okay, that wasn't true. She *did* prod him about his personal life, all the time—it's what pseudo big sisters did. Still, the less he knew about this job, the less he could tease her about it. Goodness knew, she'd already been razzed enough by the women in her family.

Which was silly and a wasted effort. The hermit was cute, she'd give them that, but that's as far as she was letting any of this go. And for good reason.

Del had learned the hard way her first year back after college that it was foolish to let her mind take a back seat to her heart, thanks to suave Mr. Jonathan Schumacher. As the red flags began to surface in their relationship, she'd pushed them away, buying into his excuses without question. And why wouldn't she when they were going on one exotic vacation after another? Ten months later, as she'd sat on her back porch daydreaming about a future beachside wedding, Mia arrived with some news she'd stumbled across online: wedding bells were in Jonathan's future.

They just hadn't been in Del's.

The shocking news had broken her heart. His betrayal had convinced Del to keep her tender heart locked away for a while. Over time, the hurt had faded, but the trust had yet to return.

So no, Del didn't date, didn't want to date, and certainly didn't need to date. Her family and friends all knew it, too. Though there was nothing wrong with enjoying some eye candy. She was single, not dead for goodness' sake.

"Great," she said. "Just holler when you're done loading, and I promise to be quick."

"Sounds good. And you're right, it shouldn't take you long to cut down the rest of that awful shrub at Manning's place. I'll be glad to see it go."

Del groaned. Why had she even bothered trying to slip one past him? Chase was practically family, after all. "Mia told you."

"Don't know what you're talking about," he said with a wink. "Enjoy your lunch date."

With that, he headed out the door. Del watched him go, chin lifted as he whistled an imaginary tune, the cocky jerk. She pounded a fist on the counter.

"It's not a date!"

ISAAC WAS JUST starting to work on a new bid proposal when a movement alert sounded from his mailbox camera. The morning conference call had run long. It took longer than he'd expected to convince the team they should start chasing app development bids slightly outside their usual market. But his message about evolving or becoming extinct—especially when they were so close to dipping into the payroll account to pay the office space lease—had eventually hit home, and the group grudgingly agreed to give it a try. Grateful for their flexibility but equally disappointed that it had come to this, Isaac had hung up and dealt with the discomfort like he always did: by digging into his work.

But as he pulled up the video stream to the security camera, his pulse quickened.

Outside, an oversized silver pickup was now parked at the end of his drive. As he watched, out stepped Delaney, looking completely different than she had last night. Gone was her soaked and muddied attire, replaced with a bright orange polo shirt, khaki cargo shorts, and low work boots. Her hair was a light auburn when not drenched, the pixie cut with its intentionally messy styling a good look on her. Today, dark sunglasses shielded her eyes.

Isaac breathed out a small sigh of relief. She would be far easier to keep at a distance today without the lure of those bright blues. At least, he sure hoped she would be.

He pushed back from his computer, the movement rousing Louie from his late morning nap.

"What do you say, buddy, wanna get some fresh air?"

He made the hand sign he and Louie had come up with for *walk*, and the bully's behind began its happy wiggle. Though Isaac missed people, Louie's slobbery grin and happy wiggles never failed to brighten his day. Wiggles turned into circles and then into zoomies. In another blink, Louie was gone, darting down the hall toward the front door. Isaac followed on a chuckle, grateful his roommate was so easy to please.

Louie really had been a trooper during their transition to Bourbon Falls. While this location was perfect, its condition wasn't the sunshine and roses Will had led him to believe. The older house hadn't had renters for more than a year, and they'd arrived to find it a dusty cobwebs-and-spiderseverywhere mess. Birds had nested in one of its bathroom vents, a few bats in its garage and attic. And the mice? They'd been everywhere.

Neither one of them got much sleep those first few days.

But professionals had quickly been called to eradicate the critter issues, and soon the pair was able to focus on settling into their temporary home. Well, as settled in as they could get with what limited furniture Isaac had brought along. It was plenty for the two of them but took up a fraction of the home that was easily three times the size of his apartment out east.

Truthfully, the empty rooms didn't bother him nearly as much as the home's dark and dated decor. While he preferred light, natural colors, Will's aunt and uncle must have had an affinity for dark brown; the color was everywhere. Dark trim, dark floors, dark cabinets, dark carpet. Even the bathroom tile and grout were a dark chocolate brown. All fixable for its current owner, which Isaac was not.

Up ahead, Louie nuzzled the lead hanging from a hook by the door, then turned back as if to say, "Hurry up already, will ya?"

"Patience, buddy," Isaac said, reaching for his sunglasses, a ballcap, and the leash. "You're eager to meet your new friend, huh?"

He snapped the lead to Louie's collar and opened the door, then stepped aside to let his dog pass. Is that what Del would become to them? A new friend?

Isaac knew he had to be cautious. Just because she hadn't seemed to recognize him in the rain last night didn't mean she hadn't had an aha moment after she'd gone home and Googled him. If she acted differently around him today, he would know she knew.

But then what? Pack up and move in the dark of night?

He glanced back at the dining room half full of boxes. At least there wouldn't be much packing to do if it came to that. Unfortunately, he doubted anywhere else he could land would be rent-free. Could he swing paying rent in Manhattan and somewhere else?

Isaac shook his head and stepped out into the midday sun. It was too soon to think like that. Clearly, all this alone time had made him paranoid. Well, that, and the whole fiasco last fall. He'd never received so many vicious hate tweets in his life.

Clueless so far to their nearby guest, Louie took his time sniffing out the perfect patch of yard to fertilize. Though the woods that surrounded their house and yard were lush and green, the sound of a revving chainsaw would have alerted any other dog of their visitor. It wasn't until they were on their way down the drive and on other side of the woods that Louie realized anyone else was there. Suddenly, the bully lunged forward with more gusto than anticipated. Isaac watched in horror as the lead slipped from his grip, Louie barreling down the driveway and heading straight for Del.

She turned her gaze toward Louie, but rather than take

off running, Del set the saw down and knelt to receive the incoming four-legged welcome wagon. Oblivious as always to his own brute strength, Louie barreled into her, knocking her clean over. By the time Isaac caught up to them, a full-out slobberfest had commenced. Beneath a happy, wiggly Louie lay a dirtied, doggie-kiss-covered, laughing Del, her sunglasses half knocked off.

"I am so sorry about Louie. He just really loves people," said Isaac, gently muscling his dog off her.

"I can see that," she said, rising to dust herself off.

He studied her carefully, watching for any glimmer of recognition. If she'd gone home last night and discovered who he really was, she was doing a good job of hiding it. Hopefully, his secret was still safe. Question was, how long could that last?

"You must hate coming over here," he said. "Every time you do, you end up getting dirty."

"Nah, I live to get dirty. Why else would I start my own landscaping business?" She straightened her shades and motioned toward where his battered shrub had been. "It also allows me to play with cool toys for doing stuff like this. Look a little better now?"

"Wow, yeah it does. Kinda makes me wish you were cutting its twin down, too."

Will would agree. He hated plants.

Which was why all the ones in their office were fake.

"Really?" She studied the monster evergreen on the

drive's opposite side. "I mean, I'm already here. If you want it gone, say the word. Just remember, once it's down, I can't put it back up."

He nodded. "Go for it."

"All right, then. Stay back, we wouldn't want Louie to get an unexpected haircut."

She stepped away from them, retrieving her chainsaw as she went. Del's movements were smooth, practiced. The confidence he'd seen in her actions last night was even more pronounced today, but rather than be intimidated by it, Isaac felt an invisible tug pulling him in her direction. This wasn't just loneliness—it was attraction, plain and simple.

An attraction he shouldn't act on, not with the massive dark cloud currently hovering over him.

She sawed through a thick outer branch and watched it fall, then bent to drag it out of the way. Man, did she have a great butt. Connected to a killer set of legs. Legs like that would look even better wrapped around—

Isaac looked away. Whether inspired by loneliness or an unexpected attraction, these thoughts were doing him no good. It'd be best to just let her do her work and go. Safer. Louie dropped his rump onto Isaac's foot with a whine, as though reading his owner's thoughts.

"Totally off limits," he whispered to his deaf dog.

Del finished downing the other bush in a matter of minutes, then paused to drag an arm across her forehead. "I'll swing back by and pick these up later if you don't mind.

Chase is gonna be needing his chainsaw back soon."

"Chase?"

Ah, so she did have a boyfriend. Del skirted the fresh pile of downed branches and started toward him, tugging her sunglasses free as she approached. Those bright-blue eyes taunted him anew.

"The other half of Oak Barrel Farms. I play in the dirt, grow and order fresh inventory, and do the books. He does the more physical stuff, like delivery and setup of our bigger jobs. Oh, and the web stuff. I do *not* have the patience for technology."

Pathetic as it was, hope lit in his chest. "Not the kind of person who's glued to the internet, I take it?"

"Pfft, no. If it's not a power tool, I can't be bothered." She took a handkerchief from her back pocket and dabbed at her hairline.

"Oh, come on. You look like the kind of person who spends all day on Twitter and Instagram."

"Yep, that's totally me." Del rolled her eyes. "*Not*. Heck, do people even Twitter anymore? I thought Brooklyn said TipToe was all the rage now."

He chuckled. "You mean TikTok."

"TipToe, TikTok. It's all just a bunch of people trying to get attention."

Amen to that...

"Anyway, I'll give you my number. Just text to let me know when would be a good time to come back for the branches." She pulled a business card from her back pocket and handed it to him. "I'm not sure what my evening's going to look like yet—still waiting to hear on the bookstore's prognosis."

"Oh, yeah, how did it go last night?"

She sighed. "Well, let's just say it was hot, wet, and exhausting."

Isaac looked away on a nod. *Mercy, woman.*

"But the leak finally stopped, and my aunt's got someone coming out today to assess it all. Keeping our fingers crossed it'll be a quick fix."

"Definitely. And hey, thanks again for taking those shrubs down. I feel so much better not having to worry that something's going to come crashing down on me when I leave."

"Sure, no problem," she said, loading the chainsaw into her truck. "And we can work on the rest of the cleanup maybe this weekend, after the ground's had a little more time to dry out."

"Sounds good. How long do you think it will take?"

Del closed her tailgate and paused to scan the long ruts in his yard. "Depends how cooperative those ruts are. A day, maybe two?"

"That's all?"

He should have been happy to hear that. Pleasantly surprised, even. Instead, Isaac felt like he was about to be thrown into solitary confinement again.

"That's my hope, anyway," Del said. "I have a feeling I'm going to be helping over at the bookstore more than usual for a while. At least until the roof gets fixed."

"Sounds like you're about to be stretched a little thin."

She shrugged. "I don't mind. It's how we do things around here."

Isaac studied her as she picked a burr from the hem of her shorts, adding another quality to his Del observations: selflessness. Had he ever met anyone so willing to give without mention of payment or recognition in return?

If only he'd taken a chance on someone like her instead of Katrina—there wasn't a doubt in his mind that things would have turned out a whole lot differently. He'd still be out east, enjoying work as usual, his amazing apartment, the coworkers he missed, and that awesome dog park for Louie. But he hadn't; he'd chosen wrong.

And then he and Will had made it worse, trying unsuccessfully to correct the social media misunderstanding on their own.

Now Isaac was stuck living in an ugly, outdated home in the middle of nowhere, his life on hold and career under the table. Needless to say, he was in no hurry to get into another relationship. Nor could he risk it, given his current circumstances. Which meant it was probably for the best that the hours he'd be working with Del were numbered.

The less temptation for him to throw caution to the wind, the better.

Chapter Four

"TWENTY-FIVE GRAND?" DEL dropped onto a chair at the bookstore. "You can't be serious."

Aunt Faye shrugged. "That was the inspector's professional opinion."

Del ran her hands through her hair. Where the heck were they going to come up with $25k? She'd expected to hear they would need a chunk of change, just not *that* big a chunk.

"Then get a second opinion, because that guy is crazy. There's no way it's gonna cost so much to fix the roof."

"Technically, you're correct. That's the price for a new roof, which is what our store desperately needs. It also includes a tear off of the existing roof—which has apparently been patched over three times—disposal of the old material, and repairing suspected rot problems in three areas because of leaks we hadn't even seen from the ground floor yet."

Del cringed. *Rot* was definitely one term no one wanted to hear. She'd had to mitigate some of that when remodeling her own home, and yes, that tended to get expensive. This also meant they needed to get a move on with this new roof before the rot spread. With winter and the end of construction season only a few months off, the clock was definitely ticking.

"What did Thomas say?"

Faye sighed. "What I expected the town's finance man to say: that Bourbon Falls doesn't have that kind of money lying around. Worse yet, the storm caused some damage over at the park as well. They're starting to wonder if a small tornado didn't form as it moved past downtown."

"So they're going to fix stuff at the park but not our roof?"

"The park doesn't have tenants who can help foot the bill like this building does. Besides, we need a safe place for the kids to play."

Del growled in frustration. She wanted to argue both points, but knew it was no use. Thomas Knoblocker might have been the most frugal controller who'd served in Bourbon Falls, but the guy was sharp as a tack. He also had the board in his back pocket, which meant what he said went.

"And our insurance?"

"Won't cover this. I already asked." Faye offered her a sad smile. "Sweetheart, Brooks Books did everything your mother had hoped it would for this town and then some. Bringing back the love of reading to families in this area, tutoring those who struggled with reading. It's had a good run, but maybe it's time to start thinking abo—"

"No." Del rose and leveled a stern look at her aunt. "We

are not closing the bookstore. Not now, not ever. We just…need to find a way to come up with twenty-five thousand dollars."

"Delaney."

The sound of her aunt's soft voice nearly broke her. It was the tone she reserved for sharing the worst of news. When her mother passed. Her grandparents.

Del's gaze shifted to the entranceway, with its sunny storefront and season-inspired display case. To the shop's rustic brick walls, to row after row of books. To her late grandmother's handmade braided rug in the children's section, where they hosted story time each week. Memories of her family were ingrained in every inch of this store, and she refused to let them go.

"We are not giving up yet." Del started for the backdoor, needing to escape Faye's defeated look before it became contagious. "We *will* find a way."

Del stepped out into a wall of humidity and felt her stomach begin to revolt. It was all too much. The storm damage, waiting all day for news about the inspection, and now the bad news. She rushed to a nearby garbage can and lost her dinner. The stench was vile, but the following feeling of weakness bothered her most of all. Because she wasn't weak, and she refused to bow to these circumstances.

But twenty-five grand?

She dragged a hand across the back of her mouth and made for her truck. There was a bottle of Scope in the center console, kept handy for moments like this. It'd been a while since her last anxiety overload, but unfortunately this was just how her body reacted to overwhelming news. At least this time there had been no witnesses.

Mouthwash gargled and knees no longer quaking, she headed out of town to cruise the countryside and clear her head. Del cranked the radio and sang along with Luke Combs. His bad luck had turned out for the better; maybe hers could, too.

Twenty-five thousand dollars.

Twenty-five. Thousand.

How on earth were they going to come up with that kind of money? As Luke sang on, she wondered if she should buy a scratch-off ticket, too.

Del spied Isaac's property up ahead and remembered the small mountain of downed shrubs she'd promised to come back and haul away. He'd texted earlier, his number unfamiliar but its message quick to clue her in: a picture of Louie with the words "Thanks for helping my human today, he's not so good with power tools." That had brought a smile amid an afternoon of fretting. Though she wasn't exactly in the mood for socializing, seeing him and Louie might be a nice distraction to her looming dilemma.

And right about now, she could use a distraction.

She drove past his place and stopped at the shop to grab their ten-foot flatbed trailer, which was perfect for hauling this kind of spoil. But no sooner had she texted to say she was heading over than a new text from him pinged her phone.

Sorry, something came up for work. Need to postpone. Let me know when might be a good time this weekend.

Del sighed. So much for that distraction she needed so badly. Between the handsome hermit and his cute bulldog, they might have been able to keep her mind off the bookstore for at least a little while.

Isaac, she corrected herself, not "the handsome hermit." If she'd learned anything this week, it was that his grouchy hermit routine was all an act. People who shunned the outside world didn't come running out in the pouring rain to make sure teen drivers were unhurt. Or step outside with their adorable dogs to check on cleanup progress.

No, after watching him interact with Louie today, so gentle and patient, Del had concluded the man was more of a softy than some curmudgeon. Funny, she'd always had a thing for men who weren't afraid to show their softer sides. And men with scruff on their face, a look he totally rocked. If he turned his ballcap around and wore it backward, though, the man would achieve the Del preference trifecta.

On an eyeroll, she climbed back into her truck. Daydreaming about Isaac wasn't getting her any closer to saving the bookstore. She stared out the windshield, wishing for answers that wouldn't come. Just beyond the meadow of wildflowers that separated Oak Barrel Farms from her father's farmhouse stood a mammoth old tree. In the fading light of dusk, she could just make out two parallel lines hanging from one of its thick side branches, connected to a flat board suspended several feet off the ground. Her favorite childhood thinking spot: the Brooks family tree swing.

It'd worked for her countless times before; maybe it would bring her answers tonight.

She continued down Elm a short ways before pulling into her family's long gravel drive, the feeling of home settling over her with every pop and crackle of stone beneath her tires. Rex looked up from his napping place on the whitewashed two-story's wraparound porch, a sign that her father wasn't on duty today and likely somewhere nearby. Del caught sight of him as she parked, down by the pond watching his new baby ducklings. He had his phone to his ear in one hand and waved a hello with the other.

If Fire Chief Stephen Brooks was on the phone, it was sure to be work-related. Her father hated phones—and technology in general—nearly as much as she did. Knowing better than to interrupt, Del waved back and headed for her tree.

The evening was still muggy, but a country breeze had picked up, keeping the mosquitos at bay while she hiked the short distance to her favorite oak. How many hours had she spent under this very tree, swinging slowly in breezes much like this, puzzling through whatever speedbumps life had put in her path? Thankfully, none before had come with such a monstrous price tag.

She reached for the swing's ropes, lowered onto its familiar seat, and closed her eyes. With a push of her feet, she was off, the old oak's thick branch above creaking ever so slightly as she coasted back and forth beneath it. As a young girl, she'd lean back, letting her long, auburn hair brush the ground beneath her. But those lengthy locks were long gone, as were those carefree days.

Twenty-five grand.

Where on earth were they going to find that kind of money? Del needed to come up with a viable answer soon, before Faye gave closing the store serious thought. She knew her aunt's words held no teeth yet, but that Faye had dared speak them was worry enough. They'd never talked of closing before.

"Why's my sweet pea look like she's carrying the weight of the world on her shoulders tonight?"

Del opened her eyes to find her father approaching, his strides steady but slower than they used to be. She wasn't the only one who had aged beneath this tree—

She halted that thought. Losing one parent had been traumatic enough; she'd never be ready to lose the other.

"Heya, Pops."

He stopped a short distance away, mindful of the swing's path. "Let me guess—you talked to Faye?"

She nodded, slowing to a stop but not yet ready to rise. Here, she felt comforted, supported. Besides, she'd come to the swing for answers and still had none. "We can't lose the store, not like this."

He looked toward the house, doing that thing with his lips that was somewhere between a purse and a pucker. It was his thinking pose, one that tended to precede carefully considered words of wisdom. "You know, when your mother first asked me to buy into that shop—"

"Simpson did an amazing job last night," she cut in, refusing to let him go down the same path his sister had not an hour ago. "We'd have never gotten the tarps in place without him."

Her father studied her for a moment. If anyone exceled at handling her boldness, it was Pops.

"Glad we could spare him for a few hours. Busy night, thanks to a few ill-placed lightning strikes and that wicked downdraft. Had to recruit extra help over at the park to make it safe again before daybreak." Her father lowered himself onto the ground and turned his gaze to the sinking sun setting their evening sky on fire. "But that's what this town does best—pulls together to help those in need."

"Exactly, which is why there has to be a way to save the bookstore. Like, a town-wide fundraiser or something."

"Sweet pea, it's going to take more than a few bake sales to repair that roof."

No doubt about that. Usually, those brought in a few hundred dollars for local charities. They needed several thousand. "You're right. So, what might work better than a bake sale?"

Her father chuckled. "I'm afraid you're asking the wrong person for those kinds of ideas."

Of course! Del needed more than ideas from the old oak tree, she needed a full-blown, Bourbon Falls meeting of the minds. And she knew just which minds to recruit. She hopped off the swing and wrapped her father in a quick hug.

"Thanks, Pops. You're the best."

"Not sure what I did, but always glad to help. Just promise me you won't touch your retirement savings."

"I promise," she said, hurrying back to her truck…and praying it wouldn't come to that.

"TWO CONFERENCE CALLS in one day—what's the special occasion?"

Will rolled his eyes. "Does your former college roommate really need a reason to call more than once a day?"

An hour after dinner? On a Thursday? "Yes."

On screen, Will raised his hands in defeat. "All right, you caught me. I do have a reason for the call."

Of all the evenings he could have picked, why tonight, when Del was due to swing back by for the downed branches? Though they hadn't planned this as a leisurely visit, Isaac had still been looking forward to it. Looking forward to having more company and actually…peopling. Something, admittedly, he shouldn't be doing.

Was that why Will had called? Some sixth sense kind of thing?

"You know, you could have just asked me to stay on this morning's call a little longer. I mean, I wouldn't want to cut into your evening plans."

Will's eyebrows rose briefly. Okay, that'd sounded a little more resentful than he'd meant it to. Though, could anyone blame him? Will was out east, probably living life to its fullest while Isaac was stuck in a sea of short, leafy crops with his life on hold.

Then again, he'd accepted Katrina's invite to coffee, not Will.

"Listen, I get that you're frustrated, but remember—you were the one who said keeping you out of sight also helps keep you out of mind."

"I know, I know. It's just..." Isaac sighed. "It sucks, man. There's no way to sugarcoat it."

"There's gotta be some perks, doesn't there? Like no Manhattan noise? No traffic? No getting interrupted at the office by people showing up in your doorway every fifteen minutes?"

"For you, they show up every fifteen. For me, they text every five." Isaac winked. "Yes, there are a few perks, and I can walk away from my phone as needed. But this glass half full optimism won't last forever."

"Nor do I want it to," Will said. "I may be the face of this company when it comes to bidding work and communicating with clients, but you're the brains and the brawn inside these walls. You left some big shoes to fill, man. Shoes that don't fit me so well."

Great, more guilt. As if spending all afternoon hunting for bids that deviated from their original mission hadn't been a gut punch enough. "You don't give yourself enough credit, Will. The staff respect you as much as they respect me. Probably more, given the hell my private life has unleashed on the company."

"They're still behind you, Isaac. One hundred percent. But, yeah, this arrangement is starting to wear on everyone. Which is why I'm happy to finally say, I think the additional PR expenditures are starting to pay off."

Now that was the kind of news he'd been waiting to hear. "Really?"

"Yes. I have a private investigator discretely keeping tabs on Katrina. Apparently, she's been ramping up her online presence by doing a variety of attention-getting schticks: pranks, rants, dares. Her following has been growing exponentially these past several months. Go figure, eh?"

Isaac's jaw dropped. "So dating me was just a preamble to some online attention grab? How does this woman have any credibility at all?" And how had he been the world's biggest sucker and allowed himself to be played by someone like that?

"Great question, and an angle I plan to explore thoroughly. If we can discredit her, it'll make our job of publicly clearing your name that much easier. Of course, we'll let the experts handle it this time."

Isaac shuddered. The press had been ruthless last fall. After Katrina publicly threw him under the bus, and he'd unsuccessfully tried to defend himself, the Twitterverse had eaten him alive.

The worst part was, he'd done what he felt was the right thing—defending that elderly couple at the Giant's Stadium concession stand from a group of drunken hecklers on a bachelorette bender. He had no clue that Katrina recorded his rant afterward to the guys in the bleachers sitting next to them. Jaded after their breakup a few weeks later, she'd trimmed it down so that it sounded instead like he was bashing women in general. Then she plastered the clip all over social media, painting him to be some corporate, misogynist pig.

#RobertManningHatesWomen

#RobertManningMisogynist

#RobertManningSucks

It was no wonder hashtags still gave him nightmares, or why women all over the Big Apple had started throwing their drinks at him while getting in and out of taxis. When the hate mail started showing up at work, clients began to pull away.

"But what if your plan backfires?" he asked Will. "Our company can't survive another derogatory publicity hit."

"Don't worry, I've got a whole team working on a way to

bring you back without torching every bridge we've built. Because while it's great that we found a way to have you work remotely, it's definitely not as convenient as having you here."

"Tell me about it," Isaac muttered.

"Look, just keep encouraging the team to go after as many bids as possible and keep your head down a little longer," Will said. "If we're lucky, this whole thing could be cleaned up by Christmas."

"*Christmas?*"

"Or maybe Halloween. Hopefully sooner."

Isaac raked a hand through his hair. How had one short relationship managed to go so wrong?

Isaac struggled the remainder of the evening with restlessness. Thankfully, it was Thursday—the one day he allowed himself a reprieve from the Island o' Manning. At eleven o'clock each week, he jumped in his Ford Escape and did precisely that: escaped from Bourbon Falls. Twenty miles to the west sat Grissom's Market, a mom-and-pop grocery store that surprisingly stayed open all night and had most of his essentials. What he couldn't find there, he simply ordered online and had shipped to his door.

Truthfully, he could have had his entire order delivered, but these weekly trips held benefits that were twofold: one, they helped support the local economy, and two, it gave him a legitimate excuse to get back out into society, if only for a little while.

No, it wasn't exactly "keeping his head down," but it was the only way Isaac knew to keep from going completely stir crazy. Plus, the store was generally empty that late on weeknights, and he always made sure to go unshaven and wearing his ballcap nice and low.

Tonight, eleven couldn't come fast enough. He had his shoes on and laces tied at five til, counting off the seconds until his departure. Silly? Undoubtedly. But then, so was this entire arrangement. All he could hope for now was that Will and his cleanup team knew what they were doing…and were doing it as quickly as possible.

By eleven-thirty, he was strolling through the aisles at Grissom's, in no hurry to find the items on his meager list. Dog food and milk were his only absolute necessities this trip, but that didn't stop him from cruising every aisle and stopping to consider each sale advertised. He slowed before the next sea of "sale" tags, trying to figure out what exactly they were advertising.

"Too many options to choose from, huh?"

Isaac spun to find Del approaching, a smirk on her perfect pink lips. "Uh, no. Just lost in thought, I guess."

"Yeah, it happens to me in this section, too." She glanced at the brightly colored packages of maxi pads, her smirk growing.

Of all the sections she could have found him in. And heaven forbid he actually have a decent comeback to her teasing jabs. What was it about this woman that seemed to scramble his thoughts every time she drew near?

Tonight, he would blame her subtle lavender perfume.

"What are you doing here so late?"

"I'm here for Seyfert's cheese puffs, oddly enough. Grissom's is the only place in the area that still carries them."

He scanned the empty aisleway. "Wow, you must really love your snacks."

"They're not for me," she laughed, the sound brightening his sour mood. "I'm using them as incentive for a friend to come by tomorrow. They're her weakness. It's kinda my version of that line from *Field of Dreams*—if you buy them, they will come."

"It takes bribery to get her to visit?"

"No, but I need to be extra sure she's there. I'm gathering all the brightest minds in town to help brainstorm ways to save our bookstore."

Isaac grimaced. "I take it the verdict came in?"

The smile on her face dimmed. "Yeah. Twenty-five grand to remove and replace the roof, along with a few rotten beams."

"Oh, man. Sorry to hear that. Insurance won't cover it?"

She shook her head. "Long story, but technically the town owns the building; we just rent the space. And even if Bourbon Falls did have that kind of money sitting in a bank somewhere, we can't expect them to put it toward reroofing an old building. Those reserves are for bigger things that protect the public, like failing roads or bridges. So, yeah, it's up to us to come up with a pretty big chuck of change. You didn't happen to bring your checkbook with you, did ya?"

"Afraid not. I'm also pretty sure even if I did, my check would bounce before you made it out of the bank's lobby."

She offered him a grin and shrugged. "I had to try."

There was a twinkle to her eyes as she said it, a subtle spark of orneriness. Lonely or not, he was finding Del fun to be around.

"Anyway, I should get going. It's way past my bedtime, and I still need to get everything ready for tomorrow's gathering."

Isaac knew he should let her be on her way, but his selfish side wanted her to stay a little longer. "Wow, just how big a gathering is this?"

"Maybe ten or so. My sister Mia—Brooklyn's mom—will help, and Brooklyn, too. But I like to have everything just right, you know?"

He did, because back east he'd been the same way. Here, he didn't have that problem. It was just him and Louie he needed to impress, and neither were very picky. "Well, good luck, and hopefully they come up with the perfect idea to help rescue your store."

"Thanks, I sure hope so. If you have any fabulous ideas for fundraisers, send them my way."

Isaac was relieved she hadn't invited him to join the party; he would have hated to turn her down. Just because she hadn't recognized him so far didn't mean he'd be so lucky with the rest of her guests.

"Will do," he said. "Oh—do you think you'll still have time to come help with my yard this weekend?"

"Yep, that's my plan. Shoot for Saturday, say nine o'clock?"

Her confirmation helped lift his spirits, even if it meant this weekend he'd be rolling up his sleeves and getting sweaty and muddy. To enjoy more of her company, he'd gladly do it. "Sounds good to me."

"Great, see you around. Oh"—she glanced over one shoulder—"and can I offer a word of advice?"

Isaac's breath caught in his chest. Had he read her wrong? Had Del discovered his secret after all? She leaned closer, her look conspiratorial.

"I wouldn't stand here, staring at this section much longer if I were you. People might start to talk."

Del gave a subtle head-tip toward the end of the aisle. Isaac looked past her to spy a little old man shuffling past, his shock of white hair barely contained by a worn fedora. The man glanced toward the two of them, eyed the colorful packages to their right, then shook his head and kept on going. Isaac dropped his head in embarrassment.

"Appreciate the tip."

Del bumped her elbow to his. "Anytime, buddy."

Buddy? A warmth blossomed in his chest. Was he beginning to be her buddy?

It was futile to deny he was lonely and homesick. Having

even just one friend here could make his stay in Indiana more tolerable. But was it wise to come out from hiding, even with just one person?

As disappointment settled in when Del rounded the endcap and disappeared from view, he had his answer. Wise or not, Isaac needed a friend. Who was he to turn away the one person fate had dropped into his life?

Chapter Five

DELANEY STOOD IN her backyard the next evening, surrounded by the women she leaned on most in Bourbon Falls. Faye was at the punch bowl, ladling their family's go-to 7Up, Hawaiian Punch, and rainbow sherbet mixture into red plastic cups. Mia was beside her with a bottle of Bacardi in hand, ready to add an adult splash for anyone needing extra brainstorming inspiration. The three guests receiving their beverages—well spiked, as was to be expected—were The Sisters, a trio of elders born and raised here who maintained a pulse on anything and everything Bourbon Falls: Margaret Harper, Barbara Thompson, and Nan Harrington. Brooklyn sat on a lounge chair nearby, playing on her cell phone. Just past her was Gina Pickett, who ran the town's Sweet Mash Diner with her husband Jimmy, and Robyn Owens, owner of the Fancy Fringes salon and Mia's best friend since kindergarten.

Her family, her friends, and her mentors. Surely, together they could come up with a plan to save the bookstore.

"Okay, so you all know why we're here," she said, voice raised as she made her way toward a seat on the back patio, pen and notepad in hand. "We've got a bookstore that needs a new roof or it's done-zo, and I, for one, am not ready to see that happen."

The others left their posts to assume seats as well, The Sisters sitting together in their usual cluster. "And how much is this new roof going to cost?"

"The initial estimate was twenty-five thousand," Faye said, lowering herself into an open seat to Del's left. "After some additional nudging by the mayor's wife, it sounds like town hall *may* be willing to cover five of that. Though, I'm not sure we can count on that to happen."

"We could get it down to ten if I threaten to get his mistress involved," murmured Margaret, the former town reporter, with a twinkle in her eyes. Those who didn't know her would never suspect the conniving mastermind behind her petite stature and puff of silver hair.

Nan rolled her eyes. "How many times do I have to tell you? There is no mistress."

Margaret's smile widened. "Don't be so sure about that."

"We're not using the mistress angle regardless." Del leveled a stern look to them both. "We need this to be a community-supported event, not a community-dividing one."

"You're no fun," Margaret grumbled. She took a long drink of punch, then rose for a refill.

"What about a carnival?" Robyn offered. "The PTO always does well with the one hosted at the boys' school each fall."

"But then ours would be too close to the school event," Mia said. "I'd hate to unintentionally steal funds from the school."

"Good point. I think we need to come up with something original, something a little more outside the box," Del said. "Pops is right—a bake sale isn't gonna bring in the kind of money we need."

"Unless we add edibles to the menu," Barbara offered. Her sisters groaned. "What? They fly off the shelves in Michigan."

"Where edibles are *legal*," Gina said. "The last thing I'm sure the Brooks family wants is marijuana funding their repairs."

"Hey, whatever it takes." Del shrugged. Mia leaned over and swatted her in the arm. "Kidding. Sort of. We'll stick a pin in that idea. What else we got?"

The group started throwing out ideas, and Del did her best to jot them all down. A street fair. A 50/50 raffle. A tractor pull. A rodeo. A hot air balloon race.

"What do you think, honey?" Mia asked her daughter. "What do you think the kids in town might buy into for a fundraiser?"

Brooklyn shrugged. "I don't know. Maybe a video game tournament?"

"Writing it down," Del said, ignoring the skeptical looks on the elders' faces. "Come on, ladies, keep the ideas coming."

Ideas started revolving around upcoming holidays: hayrides, haunted houses, a turkey trot 5k race, Christmas tree sales. Del worried the roof wouldn't last that long, but she kept quiet on the subject. So long as the ideas kept coming, they were bound to eventually land on a great one.

Only…they didn't.

An hour and a half into their brainstorming session, the group was doing more arguing about why ideas wouldn't work than offering suggestions for ones that would. Even Brooklyn had seen the writing on the wall, begging off to join her friends who were headed to a movie in neighboring Warsaw. Dejected, Del called their meeting to a close and thanked everyone for coming.

"Don't worry, sugar," Gina said, offering her a hug on the way out. "The perfect idea will come. You'll see."

"I hope you're right." Del gave their longtime family friend a tight squeeze. "Thanks for being here for us."

"Wouldn't miss it for the world."

The others followed her out, and soon it was just Del and Mia. Punchbowl long empty, they went inside to search for more refreshments. After some rummaging, Mia soon produced a two liter of Coca Cola, a fresh pair of glasses, some ice—and a new bottle of Bacardi.

"That was…interesting," she said from across Del's custom countertop.

"Is that what'd you call it? Because to me, it sounded like

a whole lotta failure."

Mia slid a glass toward her and smiled. "Patience, sweetheart. You know how this goes—everyone will go back to their homes tonight, get a good night's sleep, and ta-dah! An amazing idea will dawn on someone. Maybe on all of us. Who knows?"

"One can only hope," she said, unable to fully get on board with her sister's optimism.

"'You can't force creativity.' How many times have you told me that when you've been doing your landscape design?"

"Too many if you're repeating it back to me." Del let out a weary laugh. "And you're right. I just…I'm not ready to let it go, Mi. It's all we have left of her."

"Mom will always be here with us." Mia tapped the place above her heart. "Bookstore or no bookstore."

"But there is where I feel closest to her, you know? I can still see her standing behind the counter, wearing that patchwork apron Grandma made for her, smiling and ringing people up."

Mia leaned on the counter and smiled. "Yeah. And reading to the little kids from that rickety old rocking chair she insisted on having by the kids' section."

"Gah, that thing was so ugly. I was secretly glad when it finally broke."

"Me too! Do you remember? That was the day Mom was sick in bed and Dad promised he would go read for her."

Del laughed. "When it buckled under his weight and his butt hit the floor...he looked so mad I thought Pops was gonna breathe fire on those poor little kids. Never have seen him turn that shade of red before."

"Me either." Mia doubled over with laughter. "Dad went out and bought her a new rocker the very next day."

"I remember. I helped him pick it out. Mom never asked for anything, but I knew she wanted that fancy blue one. She stared at it in the window of the furniture store every time we had to go into Warsaw for something."

The pair fell quiet.

"We'll find a way to keep it open," Mia said softly.

"You think so?"

"The answer we need will come," she said with a nod. "I can feel it. Just like I can feel you needing to tell me more about this Isaac Manning guy."

Del groaned. "I knew this talk would be coming."

"Then you should have had plenty of time to get your answers straight."

Darn it. This was the trouble with having an older sister with a mind like a steel trap. Though, in all fairness, it was good that she had Mia looking out for her. Who else would have been clever enough to unearth the truth about Jonathan? Had it not been for Mia, Del would have made an even bigger fool out of herself with all those brewing plans of beachside honeymoons.

That memory alone was reason to take a good long

drink.

"Well, he's not another Jonathan Schumacher, that's for sure," Del said. "The guy rarely leaves his house. Though, I did bump into him at Grissom's late last night."

"Really? I'd heard he never goes out."

Del shrugged. "Apparently, hermits have to eat, too. Though, I really don't get the feeling he's an actual hermit. I mean, he was a little grouchy with us at first, but I would have been too if some teenager had just plowed into my landscaping."

Mia's eyes narrowed. "Yes, I can imagine how that might be a little upsetting."

"Hey, now, we told you eventually."

"Only because I happened to walk in on your conversation!"

Del raised her hands in surrender. "I made sure she was safe and unhurt—that was my primary concern."

"Fair enough. Continue."

She sighed. Sometimes, Mia could be incorrigible. "Anyway, each time I've seen him since, he's been fairly pleasant to be around."

In fact, last night he'd almost seemed glad to see her. Though, why she'd found him staring at the products in aisle eight she still wasn't sure. The memory of him blushing when she called him out on it made her grin anew.

"So," Mia prodded. "When do you see him next?"

Del smoothed the grin from her face and shrugged.

"Tomorrow. I promised to help correct the modifications Brooklyn made to his yard."

"Thank you again for that. Though I don't understand why you're doing the work without her. Wasn't that the original plan? To make her help and teach her a lesson?"

"Yes, but that was before I remembered she had marching band practice all day. I want to get this buttoned up so I can go back to focusing on the bookstore. Who knows how much work we'll have ahead of us with whatever the fund-raising plan will be?"

"True. But I still feel like we should contribute toward the cleanup somehow. Maybe I should tag along."

"Oh no. I see what you're trying to do here, and it's not happening."

Mia's eyes widened. "What?"

"Look, I know you worry about me, and I'm sure you've already been online stalking the poor guy, but if I didn't feel safe going over there on my own, I wouldn't. Besides, we're going to be out in broad daylight. What could possibly go wrong?"

"I don't know. Maybe you falling head over heels for another stranger with a mysterious past?"

Del looked to the ceiling. Why did her sister have to be such a hopeless—albeit now skeptical—romantic? Then again, if dreaming up happily-ever-afters for everyone else helped keep her mind off her own hurts, then who was Del to dampen her spirits?

Because that's all any of this chatter was—daydreams and fairy tales. And Del, for one, had neither the time nor the patience for such things. Not with a bookstore to save, a business to run, and her family and friends to take care of.

"Cut me some slack, will ya? That was so six years ago. Also, I think I learned my lesson on the last one."

Mia took a long drink. "I sure hope so. Because trust me, the last thing I ever want to be again is the bearer of bad news."

"And the last thing *I* want is to be the recipient of more news like that."

Memories of her dark, post-Jonathan days tried to surface but she pushed them away. That was ancient history now. Del had learned to keep the past in her rearview mirror and her focus on what lay ahead. Whether Isaac Manning was a part of that future, it was too soon to tell. Way too soon.

"And for the record, I haven't been stalking the guy online," Mia said. "Though, maybe with you spending more time over there, it's time I start."

Del rolled her eyes. "I don't know why you bother. Most of the stuff people put out there is made up anyway."

"Maybe, but it'll give me something to do when I need a break from lesson planning."

Del snorted. "We need to find you a new hobby."

"Don't knock it—this hobby already saved your butt once."

She couldn't argue with that. Still, Del hoped her sister's fascination with perusing online personas would one day fade. It just didn't seem right, spying on people through the internet, making snap judgments based on posed pictures and contrived posts.

Del, on the other hand, preferred interacting with real people in real time. It was there that people got to really know one another. Hopefully, she'd learned from the mistakes of her past and become a better judge of character. Besides, it wasn't like she was dating Isaac or anything. He was just a nice guy she was trying to help because it was the right thing to do. There wasn't anything romantic about it—she'd have done the same for anyone in town.

Rather than argue the point, she let it go. If her sister wanted to play Sherlock online, more power to her. As for Del, she had more important things to do.

Like coming up with a way to save the family bookstore.

ISAAC SAT AT his laptop the next morning, watching his mailbox cam and waiting for Del to arrive. Usually, he opted to sleep in on the weekends. But today he hadn't been able to sleep, excitement from getting to spend the day with another human waking him before the alarm went off.

There were worries, too, of course. Worries about her asking too many questions. Worries about him getting tongue-tied and sounding like an idiot in front of her again. Hopefully, between the sunshine and the manual labor, she'd keep her questions to a minimum, and he'd keep his stories straight.

Just before nine, a now-familiar silver pickup pulled into his driveway, towing a Bobcat on a flatbed trailer. Del's driver's side window was down, her elbow perched on its ledge. She texted to say she was here, then killed the ignition and pushed her sunglasses up into her hair. Isaac met her a few moments later.

"You sure you want to be out here? It's gonna be hot and sticky today."

He smiled. Though he wasn't a huge fan of either the heat or the humidity, there was nowhere else he'd rather be than out here with the woman he couldn't seem to get off his mind. "Since I don't see your sidekick today, I would think you'd be looking for all the help you can get."

"You got that right," Del said, pushing the door wide and climbing out of her cab. Her lavender scent tickled his nose as he took in her outfit: worn jean shorts and a yellow tank top advertising some chain, beachside restaurant. Both showed off her tanned features nicely.

"I totally forgot about her marching band practice," she continued, oblivious to his perusal. "No way was she going to be able to get out of that."

"Ah, yes, I remember those days."

She arched a brow. "You were in the band?"

"I was. Marched two years as trumpet and two as mellophone. Wouldn't trade those days for the world." He grinned. Friday night football games. Saturday competitions. Late-night bus rides. Flirting with the alto saxes. "How about you?"

"Me? Nah, I didn't do the band thing. My older sister did, though. She played the flutophone or something. I was there cheering for her at every home game though."

"So, you were a cheerleader?"

"Heck no," she scoffed. "I was there to watch the game and heckle the refs."

Isaac could totally picture her doing exactly that. In fact, he bet she was a lot of fun to watch football games with. Maybe if he was still stuck here this fall, he'd ask her over for one. If, that was, he didn't scare her off before then.

"Anyway, enough about band. Let's get today's game plan squared away before it gets too hot to think."

"Sounds good to me."

Actually, that sounded better than good. The more they focused on work, the less time they'd have to talk about the more recent past. To his knowledge, Del still hadn't recognized him. He hoped to keep it that way.

She withdrew a sketch from her truck that illustrated what his rental's yard once looked like. Apparently, mile-high thistles hadn't always ruled the entryway. Del directed him to focus on pulling weeds while she worked to smooth out the ruts Brooklyn had left in the storm.

"So, what you're saying is, you're putting me over there so I stay out of your way?"

An ornery gleam twinkled in those bright blues of hers. "Don't know what you're talking about, city kid."

"How do you know I'm a city kid?"

"Trust me, we know 'em when we see 'em." She tossed her sketchpad back into the cab. "Tell me you at least brought some gardening tools out with you."

He gave her a blank look.

"Or gloves?"

Damn. Gloves probably would have been a good idea, especially for handling those thistles. He offered her a sheepish shrug.

"And you asked me how I knew." She opened the door behind her seat and pulled out a five-gallon bucket. "Everything you'll need is in there. Pull the thistles, getting as much of the root as you can, and toss them in a pile. I'll collect weeds and branches on the trailer when I'm done with the ruts. Oh, and here, I almost forgot."

She withdrew another container from the back, removed its lid, and held it out in offering.

"Compliments of my sister, Brooklyn's mama. You know, for not narc'ing on us and all."

"Cookies? For breakfast?"

"Technically, some of us ate hours ago." Del popped one in her mouth. "And just so you know, there's never a bad time to eat cookies."

With that she was off to tackle the ruts in Will's yard. Isaac gathered his bucket of supplies and started for the weed patch, certain it'd be done in no time…which just went to prove how little he truly knew about gardening. Holy smokes, thistles were a pain to work with! Between stalks breaking, seed packets scattering, and roots refusing to budge, he felt like he'd barely made a dent by the time Del returned, announcing it was lunchtime.

"Already?" he asked, using the back of a dirt-speckled arm to wipe sweat from his brow.

"Time flies when you're having fun, huh?" She grinned. "I'm going to run the first load of branches over to my shop, then come back and eat a quick bite before putting down grass seed. After that, I should be able to help you tackle some more of those weeds."

"Grass seed?" His gaze shifted past her to where the tire ruts had been. Now, instead of deep trenches, there were parallel lines of fresh dirt. The Bobcat sat parked a short way off. "When did you have time do all that?"

She laughed and climbed into her truck. "Let's just say this isn't my first rodeo. I'll be back in a few."

Isaac watched her go, then tossed his thistle-stained, sweat-soaked gloves aside. This weeding stuff was for the birds.

The hermit life has made you soft, Manning. Keep huffing and puffing—that's sure to impress her.

Was he trying to impress Del? If so, he was surely doing

a stellar job of it. No tools to start, no gloves, and now he was a hot, sweaty mess.

Isaac returned to the house, got marginally cleaned up, made up some lunch, and then brought both it and Louie out onto the front porch. His bully had just dozed off beneath the porch's shade when Del came walking up with her lunch pail.

"Mind if I join you guys?"

Isaac felt like an elementary school kid getting invited to the cool kids' table. Only, in this case, it was the cool kid self-inviting to his. And yes, Delaney Brooks was very cool in his book. He offered her a smile and waved to the open chair across from him. "Not at all."

She drew closer then stopped, worry on her brow. "Is Louie okay?"

"Oh yeah, he's just sunning himself."

But her perplexed look didn't change. Isaac chuckled. "I'm sorry, did I forget to mention that he's deaf?"

"Aw, poor buddy. How do I, you know, not startle him?"

"Just keep walking," Isaac said. "He'll sniff you out soon enough."

A few cautious steps more and Louie's nose began to twitch. His head lifted off the ground, and then he was up and half-wiggling, half-trotting as far as his lead would allow. Del laughed and knelt to greet him.

"Heya, Louie. How ya been, buddy?"

Wiggles turned to pawing and slobbery kisses, but Del didn't seem to mind. Isaac watched the happy reunion for a moment, then gave Louie's lead a gentle tug.

"Come on, big guy. Come get your bone so Del can eat her lunch."

He waggled a large rawhide bone he'd found at Grissom's the other night, and Louie trod back to the porch. But not without looking over his shoulder every few steps to make sure Del was following. It seemed both men of the house enjoyed having her around.

Del climbed the porch steps and took the open seat, then dug into her lunch. They sat in amicable silence for a moment, him finishing his sandwich while she quietly devoured hers. And it was…nice. When was the last time he'd been comfortable enough to just sit and be with anyone? Isaac took a long drink of his iced tea and savored the moment.

"So what's your story, city kid?"

And the moment was gone.

"What's that?" he asked.

"You know, where are you from, how'd you end up here, all that stuff?" She took a drink from her water bottle. "I'm guessing the mellotrumpaphoning didn't pan out?"

He shook his head with a chuckle. Even subtly prying, she was still adorable. "Nope, my band days have long since ended. Not a whole lot of need for mellotrumpaphoners."

Del laughed quietly, and Isaac found he was beginning

to love that sound. Not because he was lonely and missing people, but because he was genuinely beginning to like this woman. Now he just needed to find a way not to scare her off with the truth.

"I grew up a few hours east of here," he said. Not a lie. "Once I got to college, I traded marching band for computers." Also not a lie.

"Oh," she said with a mock sneer. "You're one of *those* people."

He laughed. "Yes, I'm one of those people."

"Probably can work from anywhere doing that techie stuff, huh?"

"Exactly," he said, grateful she was helping him fill in the gaps. "This seemed like the perfect place to work in peace and quiet."

"Oh, you've got that right." Del popped the last of her sandwich into her mouth.

Damn, even her chewing was kinda cute. *Focus, Isaac. Focus.*

"So, what about you?" he asked. "What's your story? We've already established you weren't a fan of band."

"Oh, I was a fan, I just had zero musical talent." Del laughed. "Hmm, let's see. I'm sure this will come as a surprise, but I grew up a total tomboy."

"What? No. I can't picture it."

"I know, right? My mother wasn't thrilled about all the stains and tears in my clothes, but Pops seemed fine with not having a second ballerina in the house." She grinned. "He joked when I came back from Purdue with a degree in horticulture that he knew all that time he let me play in the dirt had paid off."

Isaac chuckled. "And your mom? Did she come to accept all that playing in the dirt?"

Her gaze shifted to the yard. "Mom passed a week after my twelfth birthday. Car accident, drunk driver crossed the centerline."

"Oh, wow. I'm sorry to hear that."

"Thanks. Twenty years this summer, and I still miss the heck out of her." She offered him a half smile. "I used to stand at the sink in our mudroom as a teenager, looking up at the ceiling while scrubbing grass stains out of my clothes and telling her, 'Now I get why you always sighed so loudly when I came in with my clothes looking like this.'"

"Ah, perspective," Isaac said.

"Exactly. I just needed a good dose of my own medicine."

"And did it work?"

"Heck, no. I just got really good at getting stains out." They both looked to each other and laughed.

"So, how does the bookstore factor into all of this?"

Del took another drink from her water bottle, then snapped the cap back into place. "The bookstore was my mother's idea. She was a teacher for years but didn't feel like she ever had enough time to really connect with the kids. She wanted to do more for them, for the community. So one day she comes to my dad with this harebrained idea to open a bookstore in a newly vacant shop downtown."

"And what was his response?"

"He kissed her on the forehead and headed out the door. Came back an hour later with a signed rental agreement in hand and his checkbook in the other. 'Don't go too crazy with it,' he said. It was the sweetest thing ever."

Her gaze shifted to the yard once more, and Isaac remained quiet, mindful not to intrude on her memories. Clearly, the Brooks were a loving, close-knit family. Envy unexpectedly pricked his chest. Isaac's home life had been less rosy, his parents divorced and older sister distant.

"It's why we have to save the bookstore. I can't—" Del shook her head. "Her memory deserves to live on."

"Then I hope you find a way. Oh! How did your meeting go? Did you all come up with a bulletproof plan?"

Del groaned. "It wasn't nearly as productive as I'd hoped. No one could come up with anything substantial. Then I get a phone call at three this morning from Mrs. Harper, who says her sister came up with the perfect idea: a talent show. They're convinced that if we offer a grand prize, people will come running. Personally, I think she's nuts. We're trying to raise money, not give a bunch away!"

"Hang on, now, they might be onto something. I mean, *American Idol*, *America's Got Talent*—those shows have huge followings. And they've got people lined up for city blocks trying to get in. All you need to do is charge entry fees for the acts, and then sell tickets for the spectators. If you play your cards right and advertise the heck out of it, you guys might just strike gold."

"Yeah, like we have any experience advertising something like that. And unless it's just a bunch of people from town, we can't really expect people to drive all the way into Bourbon Falls to sign up."

"They wouldn't have to," he said, a plan of his own beginning to take shape. Isaac looked from Del to the winding drive before them. She needed a way to collect and organize entrants; he wanted an excuse for her to continue keeping him company. Not the brightest idea on his part, and certainly one Will would definitely advise against, but what Will didn't know couldn't hurt him.

"I see gears turning," Del said, poking him in the arm. "Now, dish."

Isaac met her gaze. "Oh, the gears are definitely turning. Though there will be some terms and conditions involved."

She arched one brow. "Terms and conditions? This had better be good."

"Trust me," he said. "It'll be a win-win for us both."

Chapter Six

DELANEY HAD NO sooner gotten home and climbed into her clawfoot tub than her cell phone began buzzing. Mia—she had zero doubt that's who it was. But she wasn't quite ready to be grilled by her older sister on how today had gone at Isaac's, not until she'd had time to process it all herself.

What had started as a simple, one-day yard cleanup had now grown into an entryway revitalization project. But instead of offering to pay her for the work, Isaac had thrown out an even better idea, one she couldn't possibly turn down:

He would help develop the website and online presence for The Sisters' insane talent show fundraiser idea.

Since web design was a skill no one she knew in town possessed, Del had quickly jumped on his offer. As much as she hated the www, she wasn't fool enough to think a project as big as this proposed talent show could possibly succeed without using it. Plus, finding a web developer had already been on the group's to-do list.

Isaac was right—his idea was a total win-win.

Plus, their agreement meant more time for her over at

Isaac's, which, she was able to admit in the privacy of her bathtub, was a bonus. She'd thoroughly enjoyed his company today, and already had ideas for what to do with his landscaping. As for the web stuff, however, she was clueless. He said he'd be needing her help on it, but Del didn't know what she could possibly contribute. Isaac was supposedly the computer expert, not her.

At least that's what he'd told her. She honestly didn't know for sure what he did, as vague as he always was. And his whole "terms and conditions" had caught her a little off-guard, too. Who did volunteer work but insisted no one could know it was them who did it?

Maybe he had some serious social anxiety that kept him home all the time. Or maybe his job didn't allow side work and he didn't want to jeopardize his career. Whatever it was, he insisted that no one know he was the fundraiser's web designer.

Well, no one except her.

She sank a little lower into her lavender-scented bubble bath, allowing the warmth of the water to calm her mind and ease her sore muscles. They'd worked hard today getting his storm debris and thistle patch cleaned up. And despite his general cluelessness to yardwork when they'd started, he'd been a quick study, unafraid to get dirty and offering her additional muscles when hers began to tire. In fact, several times he'd had those mighty fine muscles on full display.

Either Isaac had a secret gym membership or the guy had

a nice home gym inside.

She closed her eyes and tried imagining him in today's tank top and gym shorts, working a rowing machine and glistening with sweat. Mmm. Those long, tanned arms and legs of his, extending and contracting in easy, fluid motions. His hands, firmly gripping the machine's handles.

Hands that looked strong. And capable—

"I knew you were dodging my call."

Del startled, sending water sloshing over the clawfoot's rim. Her gaze shot from the sudsy mess to her sister, leaning against the bathroom's doorframe. "Darn it, Mia. Knock next time, will you?"

"And interrupt whatever fantasy you were having prematurely?" Her sister's lips curled into a devilish smile. "Not a chance."

If looks could kill, her sister would have been six feet under. "Who said anything about a fantasy?"

Mia arched a brow in her direction, and Del sighed. It was pointless trying to lie to her oldest sister. The woman knew her better than she knew herself most days.

"I take it things went well today?"

"They did," Del said. "Better than expected."

Her mind went back to their lunch on the porch, Louie stretched across her feet and Isaac sharing his vision of the fundraiser's online presence. It was mostly stuff and nonsense to her, but the excitement that lit his eyes had held her in rapt attention. She'd already considered him to be a handsome guy, but throw in a genuine smile as he talked about something he was clearly passionate about? Something that was going to potentially save her family's bookstore?

She'd just about leaned over and kissed him.

Which would be bad, of course, accosting the hermit on his own front porch without warning. What if she'd accidentally run him off before he had a chance to work his techie magic?

Then again, what if he'd liked it?

She refocused her attention on Mia, who was watching her with an amused gleam in her eyes. "So did Margaret Harper call you at three a.m., too?"

Mia sighed. "Three fifteen, actually. Guess she must have called you first."

"What did you think of her idea?"

"You're trying to change the subject."

"Actually, no, this includes Isaac now, too."

Oh crap. The first person she talked to since making this agreement and she'd already broken her promise! But since Mia knew her better than she knew herself, keeping secrets from her older sister never worked. It was best to get them out in the open and then make her promise not to tell anyone else. Only, that didn't always work, either.

"What? How? Is he wanting to be in the talent show?" Mia lowered her voice with a brow waggle. "Does he have some amazing talent we need to know about?"

A shiver ran down Del's spine, and it had nothing to do

with water temperature.

"No, but apparently he's some computer whiz. When we took our lunch break, I told him about the crazy call I'd gotten from Margaret. He thought it was a great idea and said it'd be super easy for him to develop a website for us."

"Wow. That's...pleasantly unexpected. So does this mean you think her idea has actual merit? I mean, I know we didn't come up with any stellar ideas the other night, but a talent show? Here?"

"To be honest, I didn't at first. Though that could have something to do with me being irritated about having my sleep interrupted. But the more Isaac and I talked about it, throwing ideas out there, the more I think it might work. It's fresh, it's real, and people today *love* getting attention. Now they won't have to go record themselves doing something silly on TipToe or whatever."

"TikTok." Mia shook her head. "Sounds like you guys had quite the discussion about this. I'm almost afraid to ask, but how much would he charge us to do all of this?"

"That's the best part—it won't cost us a cent. We agreed to a work swap. In exchange for his help, I agreed to redesign his entryway landscaping. Oh, and to not tell a soul he's the one developing it. So that means you can't tell anyone, either."

"Noted." Mia paused. "Do you really think he'll be good to his word?"

Leave it to her older sister to be skeptical. They had her

cheating ex-husband to blame for that tendency. And stupid Jonathan Schumacher.

"I don't know why he wouldn't. Besides, if he tries to go back on his word, I could always threaten to 'accidentally' cut down that forest around his house. Surely, that'd scare him into compliance."

"You always did have a slightly evil side." Mia shook her head on a laugh. "Wow. Sounds like we need to bring the ladies back to fully flesh this idea out, huh?"

"That was going to be my suggestion, too. *After* my bath."

"Oh, right." Mia pushed off the doorframe with a wink. "I'll make the calls; you get back to your little fantasy. And don't think we're done talking about your hermit, missy."

Of course not. Del knew better than to think she'd gotten off the hook that easily.

"Fine. But remember—you can't tell anyone he's helping us."

"Yeah, yeah, yeah."

She watched Mia go, then closed her eyes again. Time to start thinking about the next meeting of the minds…

After she'd spent a little more time exploring that imaginary view of Isaac on a rowing machine.

"I TOLD MARGARET this was the perfect idea."

Del looked up from her notepad Sunday evening to meet Barb Thompson's gaze. The meeting of the minds had reconvened in Del's backyard at dusk to see if they might be able to put some ideas behind the proposed talent show fundraiser. She had spent the day jotting down ideas, doing her best to explore some of the suggestions Isaac had offered over yesterday's lunch. While she pondered, she'd asked Mia and Brooklyn to do some online searching, to see if other communities had done this type of thing and what their outcomes had been. Hopefully, they'd found some encouraging information. Because as much as she wanted to have faith in the concept, Del knew their small town would take a mighty hit if it backfired.

And if that happened, they'd definitely end up kissing their beloved bookstore good-bye.

"I sure hope you're right," she replied.

"I still think it's a gamble," Margaret said, on her second glass of well-spiked punch. "Offering a monetary 'grand prize' without any money in hand. Doesn't make good business sense to me."

"Because you have all sorts of business experience?" asked her sister Nan, who happened to be the only sister of the trio who'd owned and run her own shop. Bourbon's Bits had been a popular dime store in Bourbon Falls for many years, visited on many allowance paydays by Del and her sisters when they were little. "Sometimes you have to spend money to make money. Besides, we can always write something in the fine print that says if we don't get enough entries to cover the prize money, we cancel the event and refund everyone's entry fee."

"That's how they worded it in Muskegon last year," Brooklyn said, looking up from her cell phone. "And Toledo and Wetumpka. Only one of them actually had to cancel. The rest made enough money to pay for whatever they were raising money for."

"Just through entry fees?" Gina asked.

"And tickets," Brooklyn said. "They charged people to come and watch the show, too."

"I hadn't thought of that," Robyn said. "Do we even know where we can hold this event? I'm not sure the high school auditorium is big enough."

"I agree," Mia said. "Maybe we could set up a grandstand in the park. Or at the old depot."

Del frowned. "But then what will we do about seating? Renting a bunch of folding chairs could get expensive. And we have no idea how many people will come."

"Unless they pre-bought the tickets," Brooklyn said, angling for the snack table.

"Not everyone is as tethered to the internet as you are," Mia said, winking at Del. "I say we let people bring their own seats or blankets. Make it a family-oriented event. Unless you want to see if we could rent the amphitheater over in Warsaw."

"Nuh-huh," Robyn countered. "If we're doing this to

raise money for Bourbon Falls, this event needs to be *here*. That way we bring in money to support our other venues, too, like the diner, Max's bar, the ice cream stand..."

"Good point," Del said. "Though, what about the weather? We can't control that."

Mia nodded. "We'll need to come up with a backup location. Hopefully, we'll know a few days out what the weather will do."

"Except this is Indiana," Gina said.

Everyone laughed.

"Uh, Aunt Del?"

She looked to her niece, who was returning from the refreshments.

"Your phone was over here buzzing." Brooklyn offered it to her. "It's Isaac. He says it's an emergency."

The group went silent as all eyes shifted to Del. Forcing a smile, she excused herself and stepped inside, away from curious ears. What on earth could he be calling about that would be deemed an emergency? Had someone else run off the road and into his partially restored yard?

"Hello?"

"Hey, Del, sorry to bother you, but I didn't know who else to call."

Isaac sounded frazzled and out of breath. She could hear the crunching of footsteps on dry grass across the line.

"No worries, what's up?"

"It's Louie, he's gone."

"Gone?" The face of Isaac's adorable, rotund bulldog flashed to her mind. "I'm sure he couldn't have gotten far. How long has he been missing?"

"Fifteen minutes."

Okay, not hours, so that was good. Louie would probably just finish chasing whatever he'd run off after and circle back. They'd been through this with Rex countless times. "Well, I'm sure if you stay out there calling for him, he'll—"

Oh, shoot. Deaf bulldogs couldn't hear their masters calling. Del's pulse quickened.

"Exactly. If he runs out into the road before I can get to him, Del, I'll…"

Isaac's voice broke, making her decision an easy one. He'd called her for help, and that's exactly what she would give him. The others could continue the meeting without her.

"Stay by the house in case he comes back," she said, leaning out the door and waving Brooklyn over. "We'll be there in five."

ISAAC CIRCLED THE house, his heart in his throat. Why? Why had he nixed the idea of getting a damned underground dog fence? So what if he didn't own the place or plan to be here long? If anything happened to Louie, he'd never forgive himself. He prayed that between him and Del, they'd find him before anything bad happened—and that he'd made the right decision, calling her.

What had she meant by *we* would be there in five?

It'd been a little precarious, him requesting complete anonymity for the web design work when they were devising their plans at lunch. But she hadn't questioned his request. In fact, she hadn't even batted an eye. Had that meant she was good with keeping secrets or terrible at it?

A little late to worry about it now, dummy. Why did hindsight always have to be twenty-twenty?

He dragged the back of one hand across his forehead, trying to keep the sweat out of his eyes. Louie seemed to have picked the hottest, muggiest day of the year to go running off. Though, it wasn't all his fault; Isaac should have known the screen door that separated his house from the garage wasn't strong enough to withstand his bulldog's brute strength, latched or otherwise. Especially with the separation anxiety Louie had begun to develop these past few months. It was getting to the point where Isaac could hardly use the restroom without Louie trying to scratch down the door to get in. He had hoped that if Louie could see him through the screen door, it would alleviate some of that anxiety. He just hadn't anticipated that stupid rabbit hopping across his path on the way to the trash can.

Now Louie was missing, Isaac was on the brink of an anxiety attack, and the woman he couldn't stop thinking about was on her way over with extra help she shouldn't be bringing.

Maybe it was Brooklyn. Yes, that made sense. Surely, Del wouldn't bring anyone else along.

And where was that damn dog?

Isaac caught his reflection in the picture window on the back of his house, the setting sun painting his worried face in yellows and oranges. Crap, he didn't even have a ballcap or sunglasses on. There hadn't been time to grab them before, and he wasn't about to go inside and miss seeing Louie wander back through the yard now. Would Del or her accomplice put two and two together if they saw him without one of his subtle disguises? If so, would either run back into town and blow his cover?

He didn't think so. And right now, he really didn't care. He just wanted his beloved fur baby back, the one living creature he knew would follow him to the ends of the earth. The one he'd pledged to take good care of when he'd rescued him from the pound.

The one who had barreled through a flimsy screen door today and was now missing.

An approaching engine sounded in the distance, sending Isaac into a panic. What if Louie picked this exact moment to dart out of the woods and into the road?

Unable to stand there and do nothing, Isaac raced down his winding drive. He wouldn't let anything happen to Louie. Not today, not ever. But where had that dog gone?

As he emerged from the woods that acted as a natural

screen for his yard, a familiar white sedan pulled into the drive and screeched to a stop. This time Del was driving it. She scrambled out the driver's side door while Brooklyn hurried out the passenger side. Instinctively, Isaac slowed to keep a safe distance between them, wishing again that he at least had sunglasses on. Thankfully, neither balked at his appearance.

"I brought an extra pair of eyes to help search," Del called. "Any sign of him?"

"None. I have no idea where he could be."

"Damn. Okay, do you at least know which direction he headed?"

Isaac ran a hand through his hair, trying to think back. "I'm not sure. He got outside then started chasing a rabbit, who zigzagged all over the yard, trying to lose him. Last I saw, they disappeared into the woods on the west side of the yard. Toward the next farm over."

Brooklyn and Del exchanged a look.

"Rex," they said in unison.

Del started jogging in the direction of the neighbor's farm and pointed to her niece. "Call your grandpa, then head down to the ditch and make sure Louie's not in there."

"On it," Brooklyn said, her cell phone at the ready.

"The ditch?" Isaac swallowed hard. Did they mean the creek that bordered the back of his yard? The one generally full of water?

Could his dog even swim?

"Don't worry. If he's back there, I'll find him," Brooklyn said, hurrying off. "Hi, Grandpa. It's me..."

And just like that, Isaac was left alone again. He tried to stay calm, taking solace in knowing he had two more sets of eyes on the lookout for Louie. But with each passing minute, his fears only grew. What if Louie really couldn't swim and he'd gone charging into the ditch? Or if he'd taken off one way then changed directions, heading back toward town and its increased traffic? What if they were already too la—

A bark sounded in the distance.

"Louie?"

Two more barks. Isaac spun in the direction of the sound and took off at a dead sprint. Unfortunately, up ahead there was no driveway or worn path, only woods and more woods. Isaac didn't care, but the woody obstacles slowed his progress.

"Louie?" he called futilely, scrambling as best he could through bramble and underbrush, ducking under limbs and hurdling fallen trunks. "Louie, where are you?"

Another bark sounded, and Isaac swore he saw movement in the distance. He sped up, low sapling branches stinging his skin as he raced forward. Suddenly, he found himself on the other side of the woods that engulfed his yard, standing amid a sea of yellowing knee-high plants. And there, up ahead was Louie, his naughty, reckless, usually lazy-ass dog, being carried by Delaney. The second Louie caught sight of him, though, he leapt from Del's arms and shot off like a rocket toward Isaac, who knelt to receive his beloved pooch.

"Oh, Louie." Hugging him was a lost cause. His dog was wigglier than ever, soaking him with a thousand slobbery kisses. Tears blurred Isaac's vision as a tsunami of relief crashed over him. "I thought I'd lost you, buddy."

"Not today, you didn't," Del said as she drew near.

"Where did you find him?"

"Sitting on the porch at my shop." She hitched a thumb toward the next grove of trees down the road. "Oak Barrel Farms is in that cluster of trees you see, our family's farm on the other side of that. Pop's dog Rex hangs out there, and he loves it when other dogs come around. I figured the two might have run off together to roam, which probably would have happened except *somebody* ran out of steam first." Her soft laughter rang out. "That dog of yours was spreadeagle on the porch and didn't want to budge."

Isaac swiped a hand under each eye, then pulled out the leash he'd stuffed in his back pocket what felt like a hundred hours ago. He clipped it to Louie's collar, then he rose and pulled Del into a bear hug. "Thank you," he said, his words thick with emotion.

Tense at first, her body softened at his words. Slowly, her arms encircled him, too.

"Of course. Helping each other is what we do around here."

He nodded and made to let go of her but found he

couldn't. Whether from the scare he'd just experienced or the fact that this was the first real, sustained human contact he'd had in months, her touch sent a warmth through him that he hadn't realized he needed. Instead of loosening his grip, Isaac held onto Delaney Brooks like a man clinging to a life raft, waiting for the adrenaline rush to pass and him to get his emotions under control.

Good grief, was he shaking now, too?

"Hey now," she said, her voice low as she gently rubbed his back. "It's all right. We found him. Everything is going to be okay."

Isaac nodded, still unable to speak, his throat tight with emotion.

"Though an invisible dog fence might be a good investment for the future. Lucky for you, I know a good local landscape company that can sell you one."

He chuckled at her not-so-subtle sales pitch and drew back to meet her gaze. "Just a *good* local company?"

"Well, okay, an amazing one. I was trying to be humble for once."

Isaac watched her shrug as the sinking sun cast her features in deep oranges and reds. Had he ever seen a more beautiful sight? Del wasn't a supermodel. She didn't wear a ton of makeup or spend hours on her hair; she didn't need to. The woman in his arms possessed a natural beauty, made all the more noticeable by her easygoing smile, inner confidence, and selflessness. She could have easily told him no when he'd called, not come all the way out here and help carry the big lug halfway home.

"You know, I always found humility attractive."

Wait—had he really just said that aloud? Isaac held his breath, waiting for Del to pull away. Or smack him. Maybe both. Instead, she tipped her head to one side, smirking.

"Is that so?"

Okay, that was unexpected. Though this was Del—when wasn't something she did unexpected? He shouldn't be pulling her closer, shouldn't be shifting his gaze to those perfect pink lips, but her boldness had scattered his responsible thoughts further.

"Mm-hmm. Know what else I find attractive?"

Her playful gaze met his. "No, what?"

Isaac dipped his head lower, nose skimming hers. "You."

She shivered in his arms, and desire sidestepped logic. Isaac brushed his lips, featherlight, over hers. He kissed one corner of her mouth. Then the other. Del's eyes drifted shut. Permission granted. This time, his lips pressed softly into hers…

"You *found* him?"

Del's eyes went wide at the sound of Brooklyn's voice in the distance. She and Isaac both took a hurried step back from one another.

"Uh, yep," she called, forcing an innocent smile. "He was over at the shop, hanging out with Rex."

Brooklyn threw her hands up as she continued stomping

toward them, still a ways off. "It would have been *nice* for someone to call and *tell* me that. Maybe then I could have stopped before finding that slick spot and landing square on my butt. In my brand-new shorts, of course." When she finally reached them, she turned her backside toward them and looked over one shoulder. "How bad is it?"

Isaac looked from the massive mud print to Del, who was pretending to squint in its general vicinity.

"It's barely noticeable," she answered for them both.

Brooklyn gave her a flat look. "You're a terrible liar, Aunt Del. And these grass stains had better come out."

She angled for the road that would lead them back to her car, muttering about stupid, slippery ditch grass. The minute her back was turned, Del looked to Isaac, and the two burst out in muffled laughter.

"I can totally hear you," Brooklyn called.

"Sorry, B. Coming!" A blush darkened Delaney's cheeks. "Glad we could help you find Louie. I'll, uh, see you around."

"Yes, thank you!" he called as she hurried off.

But as he watched her put a comforting arm around her niece, Isaac realized she wouldn't see him around, because here was the only place he should be. Amazing as that kiss had been, it shouldn't have happened. This thing between them *couldn't* happen, not if he was going to keep his company safe.

"What was I thinking?" he said, watching them drive

away.

Louie dropped his rump on Isaac's feet with a snort.

"You're right, I wasn't." On a sigh, he hoisted Louie in his arms, needing to get them home before darkness fell and they both got lost. "It won't happen again."

Chapter Seven

DELANEY TOLD NO one about the kiss, nor about Isaac and his missing dog. Yes, she'd returned home to a waterfall of questions, but all she would say was that she had gone to lend a hand to a friend in need. And since she'd dropped Brooklyn and her car off at her home so she could change out of her muddied shorts, her niece wasn't there to say otherwise. That meant the others could do nothing but pout and scowl when she refused to give them her temporary whereabouts, which she pretended to innocently ignore.

Mia, of course, would eventually go home and get the full story from her daughter. That didn't worry Del; Mia already knew about Isaac. Even better, it was quite obvious that Brooklyn hadn't seen the kiss. If she had, she would have given Del grief about it the entire drive back into town. That meant the only two people on the planet who knew about the kiss were her and Isaac.

And oh, what a kiss! It was soft and sweet and tentative and gentle and might very well have been the best first kiss ever. The kind that left you swooning and wishing for many, many more.

Which was precisely the problem—they were doing work for one another. Mixing business and pleasure could lead to poor decisions. Sure, his life would go on if she botched his landscaping, but what would she do if things soured between them before he got their website finished?

The worry consumed her the minute she was allowed off the hot seat, and she had trouble refocusing on the fundraiser meeting. Thankfully, her struggles were short-lived. Not long after she returned, the group began to dissipate. They'd formed general ideas as well as a strategy for how to get the mayor and town board's approvals. Once the red tape was cleared, they would be free to proceed.

And free to charge ahead with the website. Which would mean spending more time with Isaac. Oh boy. Could they possibly stay focused on the web design now, or would desire overshadow their agendas? Cause delays? Lead to broken links and a crappy web—

"Delaney Brooks, are you listening to me?"

Her gaze sharpened on Margaret Harper, who'd risen with her sisters but had yet to leave. "I'm sorry. What was that?"

"I said, Mia told us you found someone who might be able to put together a website for the fundraiser. Do we know how much it will cost?"

Her worries about kissing troubles took a sudden backseat to a more immediate problem: she hadn't given any thought as to what she would tell the others about their mystery designer. Worse yet, Brooklyn was correct—she was a terrible liar. Del knew the best way not to get caught in a lie was to not tell one. Exactly.

"Nothing," she said.

Margaret arched a brow, her former reporter's gears obviously turning. "You're telling me they're going to do the work for free?"

"Yep," she said, sitting up straighter. "It's completely pro bono, their contribution toward the fundraiser."

"Do they even have any experience with this sort of thing?"

From the corner of her eye, Del saw Mia look away. Clearly, she was still hung up on the "not knowing" thing. But in all fairness, none of them could say with certainty that Isaac could do what he'd promised he would. Though she couldn't imagine him lying about something like that. It just didn't fit the Isaac she knew. So instead of sharing her worries with the others, Del took a leap of faith and hoped like crazy he'd been telling her the truth about his work background.

"Quite a bit, actually."

"Excellent," Barb said, ignoring her sister's skepticism. "Hopefully, they can make it to our next meeting on Tuesday, then, and we can talk through our ideas."

"No!"

The trio fell quiet. Del threw an imploring look to Mia, the only other guest to remain, hoping for a little help.

"Uh, what she means is, the web developer is from out of town and won't be able to attend our meetings. Which, we decided while you stepped out, Del, would be held on Tuesday and Thursday evenings over at the bookstore for the next six weeks. So, you'll just have to take good notes and relay our information to your friend."

"Oh," Barb said, her smile dimming slightly. "Well, I suppose that's a concession we can make for them to build us a free website, right?"

Del nodded. "Exactly. Wait, why are we only meeting the next six weeks?"

"Because," Nan said as The Sisters stepped out the side gate leading from Del's yard into Margaret's, "that's when we decided the talent show will be: the first Saturday in October, six weeks from today. I suggested the following weekend, but your sister pointed out this was the only weekend in early October that half the town wouldn't be away at a marching band contest."

It was true—the band did have a substantial following. But six weeks to pull this off? Del smiled through her shock, wished them a good evening, and then hurried back to her sister, who was bringing snacks in from the back porch. She grabbed the punchbowl and followed Mia into the kitchen, quick to shut the door behind them.

"Six weeks to organize something this huge? Are they insane?"

"It's cutting it closer than I'd prefer," Mia said. "But if

we push the date out past marching band season, who knows what the weather will be like."

"This is Indiana, Mi. Who knows what the weather will do *tomorrow*, much less six weeks from now."

Mia chuckled. "True. But the longer we push this out, the more risk we're taking for the roof to give out."

Okay, that was a valid point. Heck, as it was, Del held her breath every time she heard the weather forecast, praying for nothing more than a few scattered sprinkles. Still, just six weeks to pull this all off? It was gutsy for sure.

"You know, if your new buddy can't produce this supposed online signup and ticket sales website, Barb's idea may never get off the ground."

"Then I'll just have to make sure he stays good to his word," Del said.

Maybe with the lure of more kissing. To commence after the project was done—if she could hold out that long.

"I gotta be honest, I'm a little hesitant to put all our eggs in one basket here." The concerned look on her sister's face deepened. "I mean, what if he skips town or something?"

"Then we'll just have to find someone else to do the website. Surely, someone around here has at least the basic kind of skills we'd need even if they might not be as gracious and offer to do it for free. Wait—why are you so worried about his leaving all of a sudden?"

"Well..."

Del narrowed her eyes. "You stalked him online, didn't

you?"

"Maybe."

An exasperated sigh escaped her. "Then we might as well address the elephant in the room. Out with it—what'd you find?"

"That's just it—I haven't found anything." Mia threw her hands up. "Nothing at all."

"So?"

"What do you mean, 'so'? Don't you find it odd—a techie with zero online presence?"

"Not everyone loves to sit around posting their favorite memes on Facebook, you know. If you look me up, do you find an online presence?"

"But you're not a supposed computer whiz. Do you even have any proof that he does what he said he did?"

"No," she said, hating to admit it. "But the way he talked, he sure sounded like he knew an awful lot about it."

"What if he's just saying those things to impress you?" Mia shook her head. "I don't want to see you get hurt again, sweetheart."

"Great, because that makes two of us."

Her grin wasn't reciprocated. She watched Mia gather her things, unsettled that her sister was taking this so seriously. Was there more to her research than she'd shared?

"Please promise me you'll be cautious."

"I will."

"I mean it, Delaney. You are far more important to me

than the bookstore. If you get the slightest hint that this guy is a phony or bad news, you tell me, and we'll find someone else to help us."

"Fine."

Mia hugged her good-bye then left through the side door, her words still rattling around Del's brain. Mia was correct: they really didn't know much about Isaac. But Del wasn't one to judge a person by their social media presence, either. Too much of that was contrived, people painting the best pictures of themselves. It wasn't real. And though, no, she didn't know everything there was to know about Isaac Manning, what she had seen of him so far was that he was a hard-working man who cared deeply for his dog and others. That he was funny, handsome, and a heck of a kisser were just added bonuses. Besides, they needed a web person, and who was she to turn away the one who'd just fallen into their laps?

Mia just worried too much, was all. A cheating ex would do that to a person. And while, yes, Del had been burned before, she didn't plan on letting her heart get anywhere near a flame to let that happen again. They were just having fun. Heck, it was one kiss!

No, in her mind, the bigger concern of the night was the slim window of time they had to pull together this talent show.

Six measly weeks?

Del tucked Mia's warning into the back of her mind and

grabbed her cell. Surely, nine o'clock wasn't too late to text the man poised to help save them all. She sent him a quick message.

We need to talk.

ISAAC WOKE BEFORE the sun Monday morning, disoriented and absolutely roasting. Eyes open, he found himself in his recliner instead of his bed, Louie sprawled across his chest. All the drama from the night before must have caught up with them both.

On a groan, he eased the bulldog furnace off him and rose to grab a cooling drink of water before migrating to bed where they both belonged. Rehydrated but still groggy, he gathered his cell phone from the kitchen counter and shuffled toward his bedroom.

It was 4:00 a.m., and he'd missed a text from Del.

We need to talk.

Crap. Apparently, he wasn't the only one having second thoughts about that kiss. Worse yet, she'd sent it last night after he must have collapsed in the recliner from both physical and emotional exhaustion. Would she think the worst since he hadn't responded?

He sent a quick text back, thanking her again for her help last night and confessing he'd fallen asleep early, and hit send. Reading what he'd sent, he shook his head—he'd forgotten to answer her message. Isaac dragged a hand down the side of his face. Maybe he should have waited to text when he was more awake. He sent another text, agreeing they should talk about this and to call anytime. Then he set his alarm and crawled into bed, hoping to get a few more hours of sleep before officially starting his day.

His phone chimed. Man, he was out of it, forgetting to silence his phone. Isaac knew better, since he got email notifications all hours of the day. On a sigh, he reached over to silence it and found a response from Del:

Would rather discuss in person. Today is bad, can Tuesday evening work?

Great, now he'd made her mad *and* disrupted her sleep. He should have known he hadn't escaped out from under that black cloud that easily. Hoping that kiss hadn't screwed things up royally between them, he confirmed she was welcome to stop over anytime Tuesday evening. Then he set his phone down once more and proceeded to stare at the ceiling and wait.

And wait.

And wait.

No response. Either she'd fallen back to sleep or was too upset to text. Guilt rattled him as he lay in bed, now wide awake, staring at the ceiling. If the kiss had upset her, then he needed to do something more than apologize to keep her from backing out on their arrangement. Because if she did that, he'd be back to solitary confinement again. He shuddered. If the past week had taught him anything, it was that he needed human interaction, and not just via web conferences or phone calls. But what could he do to win back her friendship?

Maybe, what I do best. Research.

And he had two days to do it. That was more than enough time for him to put together a proposed web design and strategy to help Del raise the money she needed to repair the roof on her family's bookstore. Surely, that would go a long way toward salvaging what he could of their new friendship. The thought allowed his overactive brain to quiet, and he finally fell back to sleep.

HEADED YOUR WAY.

Her much-awaited text arrived at eight o'clock Tuesday evening. This time, Isaac was prepared. Wasting no time, he took a two-minute shower and changed into clean clothes, not wanting to look or smell like he'd sat in front of his computer all day. Which, of course, is exactly what he'd done; between work and research, he'd logged many, many hours there this week. Hopefully, it'd be enough.

But just in case, he added an extra splash of cologne for good luck.

When the doorbell rang, he grabbed his laptop and slipped out the front door, trying not to wake a napping

Louie. Del stood a few feet back from the door, looking beautiful as ever in a flowery top and jean shorts. Pink painted toenails peeked out from beneath her sandal straps. But the smile she wore didn't quite meet her eyes.

Yep, he'd caused some friction between them with that kiss. But he could make it right, *would* make it right. Whether or not they ever kissed again, the last thing he wanted was to ruin the one friendship he had in town. And they shouldn't be kissing, he knew, but damn, he'd be a liar if he didn't admit he sure wanted to.

"Thanks for stopping by." He motioned to the chairs on his porch, allowing her some space. "Please, have a seat. But before you share what you want to talk about, I have something I need to say."

"Ooookay." She perched on the edge of one seat.

He eased into his seat, angling more in her direction. "I was wrong."

Confusion clouded her features, those mesmerizing blue eyes locked with his. "Come again?"

"To kiss you. I just...between the emotion of having Louie run off and me worrying and worrying and then you and Brooklyn showing up and—" He shook his head. "It was wrong to cross that line with you, and I promise not to let it happen again." *Unless you want it to, which I hope someday you do.*

Her brows rose. "Oh. Well, that's very noble of you, but that wasn't why I said we needed to talk."

Isaac felt both sucker-punched and hopeful all in the same moment. "It's not?"

"No. But you're right, we probably shouldn't be kissing, because we have bigger things to worry about."

Oh, no, what had happened? An old boyfriend returned to town? She was moving? She—

"The talent show? It's going to be in six weeks." At his blank look, she leaned closer. "Six weeks, Isaac! How the heck are we going to pull together something this huge in just six weeks?"

"Wait—that's what your text was about?"

"Yes! While I was over here hunting for Louie, the powers that be went and decided October first sounded like a marvelous day to hold our fundraiser. I wasn't there to tell them they're completely bonkers."

He hadn't blown it with her, and maybe kissing wasn't off the table—even though he knew deep down it should be. Isaac was able to take his first full breath in days. He put on his imaginary consulting hat and offered her an encouraging smile.

"Actually, I think six weeks is completely doable. If you help me with the web design, of course. I can't create the perfect one without your input." Del leaned away. Why was she grimacing? "You look like you're asking me to help you remove a splinter."

"That's because for me, when it comes to technology, a splinter would be less painful."

"Did something happen with computers that scarred you somehow in the past? Like a screen toppled over on you at school?"

His attempt at inserting some levity into the moment worked. Del shook her head and chuckled, the tension in her shoulders visibly lessening. "No, no, nothing like that. I just have no patience for downloading drivers and making passwords and forgetting passwords and having to make more passwords and then losing those, too."

"Ah, yes, the slippery slope of password Hades. Those can be dark times, indeed." He winked. "But don't worry, I'll try to keep this as painless as possible. I even found a few websites to help give you some ideas of what we can do with yours."

"Really? That's great, because I'm a visual person. Too many words and it all just kinda runs together in my head. And I brought my notes from tonight's meeting with the few details we've worked out so far. But I'm going to apologize ahead of time—I haven't had time to type them, so they're kind of a mess."

Isaac grinned. After working with Will since college, he firmly believed there wasn't a scribble on this planet he couldn't decipher. "I'm sure we can muddle through. Do I need to turn the porch light on?"

"No, I think I can manage."

He let her talk, then, sharing the highlights from their event committee's past two meetings. Six weeks was an ambitious goal and could mean some lost sleep for him in the next few weeks, but he was up for the challenge. Besides, he was jonesing to work on something other than bid proposals.

When she'd finished going over her notes, he opened his laptop and began showing her various sites he had found advertising similar events. Some were extensively built out and beautifully designed; others were more streamlined and functional. He envisioned something in between, simple but one that would help attract acts from around their region.

"And this one might be my favorite example," he said, pulling up a fundraiser page from Charlotte, North Carolina. "See how clean and inviting the home page is? And the navigation buttons really catch your eye."

Del nodded as she had on each of the sites he'd presented to her, but awash in the glow of his computer screen, he could tell she wasn't nearly as excited about it as he was.

"You know, Isaac, these are all great and everything…"

"Hmm, I feel a 'but' coming on." He offered her a grin.

"But they aren't us."

"Us? Oh. No, see these are live websites at other actual locations."

She shook her head. "No, I get that. What I mean is, they don't *feel* like us. Like Bourbon Falls. If we're going to sell this event to the people around here and get everyone excited and invested in it, then we need to really make it…*us*."

Which made perfect sense—sites should always be designed with the intended audience in mind.

"Okay. So how do we do that?"

"Hmm." She leaned back in her seat, brows furrowed as she looked out across the yard. "When I'm designing landscape plans, I always try putting myself in my clients' shoes so I can see things from their perspective. Often, they have magazine clippings or pictures they've snapped from websites to show me… Wait, that's it." Del gathered her things and rose. "Come on."

"What? Where are we going?"

"On a little road trip." She tipped her head toward the driveway. "It'll be easier if I *show you*."

Isaac sank back in his seat. Was she crazy? He couldn't leave here, not without the risk of being spotted! Only, she didn't know why it would be a risk to be spotted—and he couldn't exactly tell her, either.

"Why waste your gasoline when I can just pull it up on Google Earth?" he asked, praying his suggestion would fly.

Del stepped forward, bringing them the closest they'd been all night, and gently pushed his laptop screen shut.

"Because seeing it and experiencing it are two completely different things."

Of course they were, he stewed as she sauntered off toward her truck. Heck, he probably knew that better than anyone right about now. But experiencing town was precisely what he'd sworn not to do.

"If you try to tell me you're afraid of leaving, I'm gonna have to call baloney."

"Why's that?" he asked, hating the panic rising in his voice.

"Because we ran into each other at the grocery store last week."

"But there aren't people shopping that time of night!"

She planted one hand on her hip. "I'm not a people?"

"You know what I mean," he muttered, unwilling to rise. Because leaving here would be a bad idea. Isaac wasn't just trying to protect his own hide but to keep the media focus off his business. He hid to protect his company, his partner, and his staff. If he did something stupid now and cost them all their jobs, he'd never forgive himself.

Isaac's gaze shifted to the twilight skies, his pledge of anonymity warring with a growing case of cabin fever. It *was* nearly dark. Could a simple car ride be all that dangerous?

Undeterred by his indecision, Del climbed into her truck, turned its engine over, and lowered the driver's side window.

"Come on, Isaac. Live a little for once."

"But what if—?" He caught himself before finishing.

"Don't worry," she said. "You'll be safe with me."

Strangely, he believed that. He was also sick to death of sitting at home, in a home that wasn't even his. On a sigh of resignation, he rose to put his laptop inside and prayed this decision would not blow up in his face.

Chapter Eight

DEL WATCHED ISAAC slip inside with his laptop. Why was he so averse to leaving this place? Was it a phobia? Some aversion to crowds that kept him at home and alone most of the time? But he never seemed to be all that shy around her. Especially not when he'd pulled her in for a kiss Sunday night.

Oh, wait—she shouldn't be thinking about that, not after he'd just told her straight up that it'd been a mistake he wasn't planning to make again. Funny, as she'd been telling herself the same thing all weekend. Only, coming from him, the words had stung a bit.

He stepped outside, looking skittish as a doe, and Del pushed her thoughts about kisses aside. Right now, she needed to get this man into her truck so she could show him just how special her hometown was. Once he understood that, he could build them the perfect website.

Because unlike Mia, after listening to him ramble these last thirty minutes or so, she had zero doubt this man was capable of such a thing.

Isaac paused outside her passenger door before opening it

and climbing cautiously inside. Tension radiated off the poor guy, and Del almost felt badly for all the nudging she'd done to get him there. Almost.

"Attaboy." She snapped her seat belt into place. "Don't worry, Mr. Hermit, I'll have you home in time to tuck Louie in for the night."

"Lucky for us both, he's in the middle of his evening nap." He snapped his belt into place as well. "Otherwise, he might have insisted on joining us."

"Evening nap?"

Isaac nodded. "He loves naps nearly as much as he loves food. And trust me, Louie is all about food."

"As heavy as he was to carry, I believe it."

Del turned her radio down and angled for the main road, trying not to notice the way Isaac's knuckles were turning white in his fisted hands. Whatever this phobia of his was, it was the real deal. Time to get him talking to take his mind off things.

"So, have you ever lived in a small town before?"

"Nope. Suburbs outside small cities, maybe, but nothing like here." His gaze shifted from the passing soybean fields to her. "Have you ever lived anywhere else?"

"I lived in West Lafayette for a few years, while I was attending college at Purdue. It was way bigger than Bourbon Falls. Heck, just the campus has more people than we do."

"But you came back."

"I did." She shrugged. "Everything I've ever needed is

here. My family, my friends. And—thanks to the land donation from my father and Chase's willingness to put up with me—my business, too."

Fields soon gave way to the large sprawling yards stretched beneath clusters of mature trees on the edge of town. After that came the smaller yards like hers, holding modest homes with welcoming porches and detached garages. Sidewalks ran parallel to the grid of streets connecting this area to downtown, and streetlamps stood at each intersection, providing broad swaths of light to the handful of kids still out riding their bikes.

"You've probably read all this online already, but since we're trying to get the right vibe for the website, I'm gonna play tour guide for a minute. Cool?"

"Be my guest."

"Okay, so Bourbon Falls has history dating back before the Civil War. The Potawatomi Indians had trails throughout the area, following our streams and small waterfalls. Then settlers migrating westward were taken by the area's beauty, and a small settlement sprang up. When the railroad arrived here in the mid-eighteen hundreds, our population grew by leaps and bounds. That's where we got half our name, actually—from the railroad that came north out of Bourbon Township, Kentucky. It also influenced the naming of just about everything that sprang up in the area afterward."

Isaac chuckled. "That definitely explains some of the

store names I've seen."

"Don't be knocking our venue names, buddy. We take great pride in our play on words." She winked and turned south on Main Street, slowing in front of a squatty, white brick building. "If you ever decide to venture out during normal business hours, the Sweet Mash Diner has the best food in town. Jimmy and Gina Pickett own the place, and they're phenomenal cooks."

"Let me guess," he asked, peering into the storefront's wide windows. "Friends of yours?"

"Longtime family friends. Plus, my sisters and I all cut our teeth waiting tables there in high school. Also, if you're into cobbler, they have the best."

"I'll have to check it out."

She didn't see that happening but kept mum on the subject.

"Just past that you'll spy the Tipsy Barrel, owned by Max Williams. He was in my sister Mia's grade in school, always a good guy and runs a clean bar. They expanded last year to add a distillery out back and have come up with their own brand of bourbon, which they bottle with a variety of flavor infusions. If stores outside our region ever pick up on them, Max is going to be set for life."

Del paused at a four-way stop, allowing Isaac time to take in the two-story brick building, painted barrel brown. The bar's blue neon sign hung off one corner of the building, the words "Tipsy" and "Barrel" flashing at offset intervals. As usual, the place was packed.

"His bourbon's that good, huh?"

"Oh yeah. But you've gotta watch yourself—it'll sneak up on you right quick."

Isaac chuckled. "Duly noted."

"Since I didn't figure you'd want to go in anywhere tonight, we're going to continue south. I do, however, need to make one quick stop."

She offered him a devious grin and eased into a tiny parking lot on the street's west side. Before he could argue, she raised a hand. "Don't worry, you can stay in here. Just tell me what you want, and I'll bring it to you."

Isaac's worried gaze shifted to the tiny lean-to across the small gravel lot, then to the large two-dimensional ice cream cone hoisted overhead.

"Frosty Falls is a staple here in the summer, and some of the best ice cream around." She paused as Isaac's stomach let out a loud growl. "And don't even try to tell me you don't want anything."

He grinned for the first time since getting in her vehicle. "Oh no, I never turn down ice cream."

"Excellent. So what are you craving tonight?"

"Not sure. What's your usual go-to item here?"

She squinted toward the order counter. "Depends on what I'm in the mood for. Sometimes it's a chocolate malt, but tonight I'm thinking a twist cone."

"A twist cone sounds perfect."

Isaac reached for his wallet, but Del waved him off.

"Oh no, this one's on me. Consider it payment for pain and suffering, since I dragged you out of the house and all."

With a grin, she slipped out the driver's side door and angled for the ice cream stand. Even at this hour on a weeknight, a small line of people waited to place their orders. Hopefully, she wouldn't be gone too long—poor Isaac was likely on the brink of a mini panic attack. Seriously, she'd never met anyone like him before.

But as quirky as he could be at times, he'd earnestly listened when she was telling him about the fundraiser decisions made so far. The research he'd done ahead of their talk tonight had also blown her away. Then there was his whole speech about how he shouldn't have crossed the line with her on Sunday.

Darn it. She hadn't meant to let her thoughts go down that path again tonight after his little confession earlier. Kind of hard not to, though, sitting mere inches from him and that amazing cologne of his. If the guy really didn't want them to do more kissing, he shouldn't have worn that cologne.

Unless maybe what he'd said back on the porch and what he wanted were two completely different things.

Mia's words of warning tugged at Del but she pushed them aside. What harm could a little kissing possibly do?

She ordered two twist cones and headed back to share with her hermit, who cracked his door mere inches to receive the offered cone.

"Thank you," he said, pulling the door quickly shut.

Del just shook her head. His behavior was amusing if nothing else. Inside the cab once more, she gave him an imploring look. "Well?"

"Thank you, again."

She laughed. "You're welcome, but that wasn't what I was asking. Have you tried it yet, or were you too busy being paranoid?"

He cast a wary glance to the parking lot. "Uh..."

"Stop staring and start eating, will ya? I'm telling you, this is the best ice cream around."

He raised his cone in toast, then took a nibble. Isaac's eyes widened. "You weren't kidding. This is really good."

"Told you so." On a wink, she started her truck.

"We're not eating here?"

"Nope, need to continue on before the coach turns back into a pumpkin. And don't you even suggest that just because I'm a woman I can't drive and eat at the same time."

He chuckled. "Wouldn't dream of it. So where are we headed?"

"Just a few more spots, but all important parts of our town's history."

Del continued with her tour guide duties in between bites of ice cream, pointing out their historic post office and Robyn's salon. Just past their town hall, she pulled into a parking space before yet another two-story brick building.

The recently updated oil-lamp-looking streetlights along Main Street cast its two storefronts in a warm glow: Haines Hardware and Brooks Books.

"This is your bookstore?"

"It is," Del said, pride swelling in her chest.

Even in the dark, their store looked warm and inviting. Her father had painted the front door blue years ago, and later the casings around the wide windows on either side holding their storefront displays. This month, the right display housed her mother's treasured—and now retired—blue rocking chair in the far corner. A beautiful, rainbow-colored quilt made by Barbara Thompson was draped over its back, and Dr. Seuss books were scattered throughout the space. To their entrance's left, Faye had placed a small wooden table in the display window, helping showcase books geared toward adult readers. Though the shop's interior lighting was off, the streetlamps illuminated far enough into the store to show a glimpse of the handcrafted shelving units.

"I can see why you're working so hard to protect it," he murmured, squinting into the darkness. "It's beautiful."

"Thank you. And it is a lovely store, but that's not the only reason we need to keep it open. For my mother, this store was her dream. Our family has worked tirelessly since her passing to keep that dream alive. Aunt Faye, my dad's only sister, moved back after the accident and picked up Mom's torch. Without her, Brooks Books would have never survived."

"And who is that?"

Del followed Isaac's gaze to the rotund orange tabby cat that'd emerged from the darkness and taken a seat beneath the display table. He looked toward them and, unimpressed by their presence, began grooming the base of his tail, one hind leg lifted as best he could around a very round belly.

"Oh, Felix." She groaned. "That's quite a first impression you're giving Isaac."

"That's all right," he said with a laugh. "I'm sure he can't see us."

Del snorted. "Oh, I'm sure he can and just doesn't care. We found him as a kitten, meowing at the backdoor years ago. Aunt Faye brought him inside to be our mouser, and he's been king of the shop ever since. We do love that fatty cat."

Felix shifted to lay on his back, feet dangling in the air like a bloated racoon laying on the side of the road. Del could only hope this view wasn't what would stick with Isaac when he was building their website. She turned to say as much, but stopped when she found him studying her.

"What is it?"

"This store really means something to you, doesn't it?" he asked quietly.

"No." Her gaze shifted to the rocking chair. "It means everything to me."

His free hand found hers and gave it a squeeze. "Then I know you'll—"

A knock sounded at her driver's side window.

Isaac froze, wide-eyed. If he'd been acting timid as a doe earlier, now he was one trapped in a set of headlights. Had bringing him out here been a bad idea after all?

"STAY CALM," DELANEY said, her words as effective as telling a man on fire not to mind the heat. "Tinted windows, remember? It's going to be all right. Let me just take a quick peek so I'll know the best way to get rid of them."

Isaac nodded, quickly scanning the inside of her cab. No blanket, not much of a back seat. Where was he supposed to hide?

She turned slowly and squinted out her window. "Oh boy. We might be in some trouble."

"Really?"

Damn. He never should have opened his door at the ice cream place. Someone had to have seen him. Heck, there was probably an angry mob forming outside right now.

"Yeah," she said, reaching for the power window button. "You might want to duck or something, just to be safe."

Heart racing, Isaac unbuckled his seat belt and bent at the waist. It was like being back in NYC all over again. The only thing missing was the sound of Starbucks cups hitting the windows. And great, now his ice cream cone was starting to melt. He licked at it as best he could in that position, trying not to drip all over Del's floormats.

Her driver's side window motor sounded, and Isaac held his breath, waiting to be discovered. Man, he knew coming into town had been a bad idea. What really sucked was that it had been going so well up until now. He should have known better to think his luck had finally changed for the better.

"What are you two doing out here this time of night?" Del asked.

Okay, two was better than a large mob.

"Mrs. Harper said she was craving a sundae, so she sent us down here to get her one."

Wait—was that Brooklyn's voice? Isaac lifted his head just high enough to catch a glimpse of her familiar ponytail. Del met his gaze and winked. *Sonofagun.* She'd been messing with him the whole time.

"You mean, she sent you down here to spy on me," Del said, amusement in her voice.

Teenage laughter followed. "Yeah, maybe that, too. But she gave us money to get ourselves something, too, so we figured why not. Hey, Isaac."

Well, no sense in hiding any longer. He tugged his cap lower and straightened, hoping whoever the friend was with her wouldn't recognize him either. "Hey, Brooklyn. Thanks again for your help the other night."

"No prob." Her gaze shifted back to Del. "So can I borrow two bucks? I thought Mrs. Harper gave me a ten, but it's only a five so we're a little short."

"How about I give you five bucks, and you tell Mrs. Harper you didn't see us?"

The teens exchanged a smirk. "Deal."

Isaac finished his cone and fished a five from his wallet. "Since you got the ice cream, how about I cover the bribe?"

"Works for me," Del said.

The girls thanked them and turned for the Frosty Falls, promising they wouldn't tell anyone they'd seen Del and Isaac in town. Shaking her head, Del rolled the window back up.

"Gotta love small towns," she said, polishing off her ice cream cone. "Your color's coming back, so that's a good thing. For a minute there, I thought I was gonna need to call Pops and have him bring the defibrillator."

Isaac snorted. "For a moment there, I thought I might really need one. We should probably get going before Mrs. Harper comes down here to spy on you herself."

"I wouldn't put it past her, though she means well. Also, she's my neighbor and an insomniac, so I'm used to her spying on me." Laughing, she reached into her center console, extracted a pair of wet wipes, and handed him one. "Can I ask you something?"

He mentally cringed, knowing what was coming next.

"Why are you so worried about being seen all the time? Tell me you're not some fugitive on the loose."

"Definitely not. And I just…" He shook his head, hating

that he'd guessed correctly and couldn't tell her the whole story. But he'd been rehearsing these lines for a while now in case he found himself in exactly this type of conversation. "I got burnt out last year, needed to get away from the big city and all of its hustle and bustle, you know? But the longer I've been working from home, the more anxious I am being around people again."

She gave him a dubious look. "Except me."

"Yeah," he chuckled. "It confuses me, too. But I think that's why I enjoy being around you—there's something about you that makes me feel free to be…me."

"Huh."

She studied him a moment, and Isaac tried acting as normal as possible. Inside, though, he was holding his breath, hoping she would accept his answer and let it go. It was best for them both to keep her in the dark and away from his drama. But he wasn't lying about enjoying being around her. He did, far more than he should.

"Well, I'm glad you feel comfortable around me. Funny, I feel the same way about you." She shrugged. "So do you need to get back to your place, or do we have time to continue our tour?"

He looked out his passenger window and blew out a silent exhale of relief. "No, we have time."

"Good, because there's one more place that I'd like to show you. Might help with your web design inspiration." She threw him a grin. "If you're not too traumatized from our encounter with Brooklyn, that is."

"Yes, very funny, telling me to duck and all." He shook his head, imagining how ridiculous he must have looked. "But if you promise not to have anyone else jump out and surprise me, I think my heart can take it."

"They didn't jump!"

Laughing, Del continued her drive south through downtown then headed west, eventually pulling into a gravel lot beside a very old building.

"And this," she said, shifting into park, "is one of the town's most iconic sites—the original Bourbon Falls Train Depot. It's actually listed on the National Register of Historic Places. The old depot gets quite a few visitors each year from historians to travelers passing through, so the parks department makes sure to keep its grounds nice and tidy. You can see they've laid newer tracks just south of here, but nothing ever went in on its north side, which means we have plenty of room for—"

"A talent show?"

"Bingo." She gave him a wink. "No one out here but us this time. Wanna see it close up?"

Isaac scanned the area, trying to confirm they were the only ones around. Truthfully, he did enjoy sightseeing, when he wasn't busy hiding from the world. "I don't know. Maybe?"

"Trust me, the only souls who come here this time of night are teenagers sneaking out or the ghosts that haunt this place."

"Ghosts?" he said. "Then maybe we should add hermits to the list."

Her smile broadened, giving Isaac the courage to follow her outside.

A lone light hung from a nearby utility pole, illuminating the entrance to a chained-off area and an aged placard containing verbiage on the depot's history. Inside the chains stood the old wooden depot, paint peeling from its white-washed siding above a crumbling, stone block foundation. On the depot's far side were the skeletal remains of what appeared to be its original covered boarding platform, which stretched maybe thirty feet alongside an abandoned rail line.

"It's like taking a step back in time," Isaac murmured, peering into the shadows.

"Welcome to a decade before the Civil War. Cool, huh?"

"Very."

They walked around the site, her leading the way and him in no hurry to leave. With no one else here, this was exactly the kind of fresh air he'd been hoping to find. Maybe if he could figure out how to get here, he'd come back again with Louie. After dark, of course.

"Do you think this helped tonight?" Del asked. "The tour?"

"I do." He scanned the depot, then shifted his gaze toward the soft glow of lights coming from downtown. "Before, it was just me driving through a cute little town.

Now I have some perspective about why it's so cute."

She turned to him, eyes narrowed. "You think my hometown is 'cute'?"

"Sorry, quaint. Unique. Is that better?"

"Such a city kid. Come on," she said, motioning toward a nearby picnic table sheltered beneath a tree with long, arching branches. "We can sit over here while we strategize."

"Strategize?"

"Or make out." She shrugged. "I figure I'll leave that decision up to you."

Isaac swallowed hard. He'd nearly broken his pledge in the truck a few minutes ago; her raw honesty about the importance of her family bookstore called to him. But then Brooklyn had arrived—again, now that he thought about it—and maybe it'd been divine intervention.

Now, he wasn't so sure.

He followed her to the picnic table, where she sat and patted the seat beside her. Moonlight was all they had to illuminate the area here, diminished further by the tree's canopy overhead. Isaac took a seat in the intimate setting, his leg accidentally brushing against hers. The unexpected touch left him craving more.

"Kinda wishing I hadn't pledged not to kiss you again."

"Oh?" She shifted to straddle the bench, her knees brushing against his.

"I mean, that'd be the right thing to do, of course. Keep business and pleasure...separate."

"What if we both promised to hold up our end of the bargain no matter what? Does that make it easier on your conscience? 'Cuz I'm thinking it'd make it way easier on mine."

She leaned closer, her floral fragrance and boldness undermining his resolve. Isaac shifted to face her. Forever may not be in their future, but he'd be a fool to let this moment with her slip through his fingers. He ducked to trace the shell of her ear with his lips.

"I promise," he whispered.

She shivered in his arms. "Me too."

"But if you don't want me to kiss you," he murmured, "just tell me to stop."

Taking her silence as permission, Isaac kissed his way across her cheek. Her eyelids drifted shut as he pressed a featherlight kiss to one corner of her lips. Then the other. Her hand slid up his chest to cup his cheek, and desire flooded his veins. He eased closer, pressing his lips softly to hers once. Twice. Three times.

The next kiss, she opened to him and Isaac willingly followed, his tongue beginning a careful dance with hers. He placed his hand to the small of her back and deepened the kiss; a small mewl escaped her. Isaac drew back, afraid he'd pushed too far, too fast. Del opened her eyes.

"Did you hear me tell you to stop?" she asked.

"No."

Grinning, she reached her arms around his neck, sidling closer. "Then by all means, don't."

Chapter Nine

ISAAC SAT DUTIFULLY at his computer Thursday morning for a project update video chat, second cup of coffee in hand and bully resting soundly on his feet. He was short on sleep again today, having stayed up late high on adrenaline and excitement the past few nights—adrenaline from all the kissing he and a certain local landscaper had been doing, and excitement over the new website he was designing for her. Which, she would soon be happy to know, was coming along nicely.

It'd been brilliant, her idea to take him on a tour of Bourbon Falls the other night. Sure, he'd driven Main Street a time or two on his own, but without her narration, the small town looked like any other he'd passed through over the years. And he'd have never ventured far enough to find the old train depot, which had been a huge inspiration for his current web design.

Del had stopped over last night to help review some of his general website layout ideas, but he had yet to show her the new depot design—partially because it wasn't ready and partially because they'd soon lost focus and gone back to kissing. And damn, was that woman an amazing kisser. When she'd nipped his lower lip last night, he'd about lost control...

"Hey, Robert, stop daydreaming and answer the question already."

He took a quick drink of coffee and blinked the vision of Del away. "Sorry, everyone. Late night, and my coffee hasn't quite kicked in yet."

"Late night?" teased AJ. "What was her name?"

Isaac forced a laugh, the question hitting too close to the truth. "You know I don't name figments of my imagination."

The group burst into laughter, allowing him to release a silent sigh of relief.

"What was whose name?" asked Will, who'd just joined the call.

"Isaac's imaginary girlfriend," Vivvy offered. "She's got him all distracted this morning."

More laughter followed from everyone except Will.

"Can we get this party started already?" Isaac asked, working to keep his voice light. He could see the gears turning in his partner's head and did not want Will thinking on Vivvy's joke too long. "I have a nap to get to. Wouldn't need it if I hadn't been up late fixing all you all's sloppy coding."

A round of groans and "whatever"s arose, but it worked; Sam kicked off the meeting and away they went. Isaac did his best to stay focused, but he kept a close watch on Will's features. His partner definitely wasn't his usual bubbly self today. If Isaac had been out east, he could have easily pulled him aside and asked what was up. Being several hundred miles to the west made that a little more difficult.

"Great work, team. Sounds like we're staying on top of our deadlines and keeping bugs to a minimum. Sam, Vivvy—I want an updated beta completion estimate by tomorrow afternoon. Monique and AJ—work up a testing schedule and get that to me before end of business tomorrow as well," Will said. "Robert—stay on the line, I've got a few more things to review with you."

Yep, something was definitely up. Isaac tried not to overthink it—he'd find out as soon as the others logged off—but his mind had other plans, racing off in all directions. Did they lose another client? Were they behind on rent?

Was Katrina on the warpath again?

Isaac silently wished the others would hurry up and go as worry laced tighter around his chest. Not soon enough, Will finished working out some printing details with Carmen and then it was just the two of them.

"Okay, spill," Isaac said. "What's up?"

"I've been waiting to ask you the same thing. You've been acting differently lately."

"I have?" Isaac frowned.

"Yeah," Will said. "You seem…happier."

He laughed. "And that's a bad thing?"

"It is when I know how miserable you were a week ago," Will said, his knowing gaze piercing him through the screen.

"So what you're saying is you want me to be more miserable? Thanks a lot."

"You're really not going to tell me what's going on out there?"

"There's nothing to tell. I'm sitting out here in BFE, working up bid proposals like we'd agreed I would do." Isaac raised his notepad into the camera's view. "In fact, I've been more productive lately than when I was sitting in the office. So if you've got a beef with something I'm doing, say it already."

"Look, I know you're sick of sitting out there by yourself, but if you want this plan of yours to succeed, you've got to stay the course. Stay hidden. If you show back up in the headlines somewhere..." Will shook his head. "I don't know how much more damage control we can handle. I mean, we're doing our best to snuff out fires the second we see a spark, but we haven't caught them all. Because of that, we're basically donating nonbillable hours on upgrades to keep the rest of our high-profile customers from jumping ship. We're bleeding money, man, and I can't seem to make it stop."

Isaac pictured their team all working extra, donating hours from their lives to keep the company afloat. Monique working from a laptop at her kitchen counter while trying to chase two toddlers through their apartment. AJ giving up time with his aging father and their motorcycle restoration project to debug new code. His flash of temper quickly shifted to the sting of shame. It was easy to forget that he wasn't the only one affected by this mess—a mess he'd gotten them all into, even if it was unintentional.

"You guys shouldn't have to be taking on extra work because of me. What more can I do to help?"

"Just promise me you'll be smart."

"I'm always smart," he insisted, but the answer sounded more like a grumble. Deep down, he knew driving into town with Del the other night had not been smart, nor was having her over yesterday, or whatever days she'd be visiting in the future. Even so, there were more days planned, black cloud be damned.

His partner smirked as though he'd heard Isaac's thoughts. "Then at least promise me you won't do anything stupid."

"Thanks for the reminder, but I think I already learned that lesson the hard way. What's the status on your idea to reveal Katrina for the vicious nut that she is?"

"I think we made some more progress this week. She's gone quiet on Twitter and ventured onto TikTok, posting clips openly criticizing couples at a mall in Philly. Commentors are beginning to call out her bullshit. If that keeps up, she'll lose credibility all on her own and we won't have to do anything but sit back and wait."

"You know, I'd almost feel sorry for her if she hadn't

tried ruining my life."

"Not me, man," Will said. "That girl has been trouble from the start. Karma can't find her soon enough."

Isaac's phone buzzed. He looked down to find a new text message from Del.

Hey there! How'd your meeting go?

He resisted texting back and looked up to find Will watching him closely. Yep, he still had his doubts. Knowing each other for as long as they had, Isaac really couldn't blame him. Though, in all fairness, if the shoe had been on the other foot and it'd been Will who'd been told to isolate, that plan might have lasted a few days, not months.

"Well, I wish I'd seen the red flags as quickly as the rest of you had. Then maybe we wouldn't be in this mess."

Will chuckled. "Next time you consider going out on a date, run it by us first. I'm sure we can vet a much better candidate for you."

"I'll be sure to keep that in mind," Isaac said, his mind instantly shifting to Del, an amazing woman he'd found all on his own. Thanks to Brooklyn's driving, anyway.

Louie chose that moment to let out an extra loud snore, which sent Will laughing across the line. It was good to see him smiling again, the stress at least temporarily gone from his features. Will was like a brother to him, their team, his extended family. Isaac silently vowed to keep their dreams alive and company safe, even if it meant cutting things off with Del.

He just really, really hoped it wouldn't come to that, because she truly was amazing.

DEL LEANED SUBTLY away from the cash register to skim the latest text from Isaac, feeling like she was back in high school sneaking notes behind her teacher's back. She hadn't dared to tell Chase about this week's developments, knowing it would get straight back to Ms. Worrywart Mia. Though, with as many messages as they'd been sending to each other today, her business partner would pick up on it soon enough.

Join me for dinner?

Oh, how she wanted to! Unfortunately, it was Thursday and she was due to be at the bookstore by six. She worked to keep the disappointment off her face as she returned her attention to one of their oldest, most loyal customers.

"Here's your change, Mr. Rivers. I promise, the missus will love her new jade plant."

The little old man across from her shrugged, his bushy white brows drawing together. "One can only hope. How was I to know that other one didn't need a good, daily watering?"

"Maybe save those 'watering' habits for the patch behind the shed instead of Maude's flowerbed next time, huh?" Chase said with a wink. "Here, I'll help you get it safely out to the car."

He tapped his watch and pointed to Del, then lifted the beautiful potted succulent from the counter. "Tick tock, girlie. Time for you to bust out of this joint so you can make your date with the Dr. Seuss gang."

She glanced down to find it was quarter after five. How had she been texting all afternoon and managed not to notice the time? "Shoot, you're right, it is getting late. Are you sure you'll be okay locking up without me?"

"I don't know. How do I lock the front door again without setting off the alarm?"

She looked at him through narrowed eyes. "Smartass. And here I was going to offer to bring in donuts tomorrow."

"Donuts? I take back whatever sarcasm I just threw at you. Also, if you do that, I'll bring in my special coffee."

Del's mouth began to water. Chase had a coffee-of-the-month subscription, and his latest delivery had included an amazing one neither of them could pronounce. Something with chocolate and spices and a few hundred extra mgs of caffeine—it was Heaven in a cup.

"Deal. See you in the morning."

She texted Isaac back from the cab of her truck, thanking him for the offer but letting him know it'd have to be another time.

How about tomorrow? Pizza delivery, my treat.

She grinned, then caught a glimpse of her reflection in the review mirror. Yep, giddy as a schoolgirl. And for once, not a bit ashamed about it.

You're on. I'll text after the meeting to let you know how it went.

Donuts and special coffee in the morning, and pizza with her handsome hermit in the evening? She could hardly wait for Friday to arrive.

One quick shower, change of clothes, and inhaled sandwich later, she was walking in the back door of Brooks Books, right on time. And, yes, still giddy. The others were already there, their voices carrying from the back meeting room as Del paused to silence her phone before joining them.

"Well, I for one, think it's fantastic," Gina was saying. "Who cares if the guy never leaves his house? At least we know this one isn't running off with other women every other weekend."

"But how do we really know what he does?" Mia replied. "Maybe he sleeps all day and goes clubbing all night? I don't want her running into any more surprises."

Great, it seemed she and Isaac were the topic of tonight's pre-meeting conversation. Del felt her cheeks warm. So who had blabbed—Mia or Brooklyn?

"Sweetheart, we know you love your sister, but she's a grown woman able to make her own decisions," Robyn said. "And have you seen how happy she is lately? Don't let your worries steal that from her."

Mia sighed. "I know, I know. It's just—"

"Hard. We know," Faye said. "But sometimes you just need to have a little faith."

"Uh, you know she's standing in the hall, don't you?"

Del grimaced. Leave it to Brooklyn to be blunt and blow her cover. She mouthed "thanks a lot" to her niece as she walked into the room. Brooklyn offered her a devilish smirk and angled for the front of the store.

"Don't worry," Del said as she took her seat at the table, "there's no engagement party planned yet."

"Of course not," Nan said. "You'll be the sister to elope. That's what the cards keep telling me, anyway."

Margaret frowned. "Then put your Pokémon cards away, you nut. Del's not eloping."

"Nor is she getting married or even dating anyone," Del added, throwing a warning look at them all. "I don't need the gossip mill churning."

"Of course, of course," Barb said. She leaned closer to Del and asked not so quietly, "But are you using protection?"

"Whoa—we are not having this conversation right now. Or ever." Del shook her head with a laugh. "Besides, if we don't get this meeting started, I'll never get out of here and even have the chance to get laid."

"*Delaney*." Faye looked to the ceiling for heavenly guid-ancc.

"The girl has a point," Margaret said. "And goodness knows this town has a shortage of babies right now. It's our duty to hurry this meeting along so we can all improve our odds."

Del dropped her head into her hands on a groan. Thankfully, Mia stepped in and took control of the meeting, shifting focus back to the bookstore they were there to rescue. Soon everyone was taking turns giving updates on their assigned tasks.

"How's the website coming along?" Mia asked, doubt etched in her features.

"We've worked out the theme and overall concept. Now it's just a matter of the designer putting it all together."

Barb patted Del's hand. "It's okay, honey. You can just say Isaac."

Del threw Mia a dark look and started to object, but Margaret cut in on a shrug. "Don't blame her, we did our homework. And since no one else in town has that particular skill set, clearly, it's your new boy toy. Don't worry, we'll keep your little secret. For now, anyway."

Great, she'd already managed to break the one promise she'd made to Isaac—not that she planned to tell him. Hopefully, he could just go on with his design work and the chatty Cathys in here would keep their mouths shut. Though it did make her wonder how big a deal it would be if his secret did slip out. Surely, the guy wasn't some serial killer on the lam.

Part of her wanted to know his story and why he'd moved here, behaving the way he did. The other part of her wanted things to stay exactly the same, moonlight kissing in ignorant bliss. Though, ignorant bliss was exactly how she'd gotten into her last relationship debacle. It was also a trap she'd vowed to never fall into again. Silently, Del conceded that maybe it would be wise to get to know him better before things went any further between them.

The discussion continued without any further ribbing, their group's optimism riding high. And though skeptical of this entire talent show idea initially, Del was starting to believe they just might pull it off. Even Mia was smiling and engaged, which always made functions like this that much more fun; worrywart or not, she had a huge heart and a contagious smile.

The meeting let out a short while later, each member leaving with a fresh to-do list. Del hugged her friends and family good-bye, then headed for her truck. A quick glance at her phone found a waiting text from Isaac.

Hope your meeting went well. Looking forward to our dinner tomorrow.

She glanced at her dashboard clock, wishing tomorrow was already here but grateful she had time to go home, relax, and get a good night's sleep before then.

Great meeting tonight—

A knock sounded on her window.

Del jumped in her seat, then softly cursed as she tried to capture her bobbled phone. Mia stood outside her door, a repentant look on her face.

"What's up?" Del asked, rolling her window down.

"Nothing really, I just… I wanted to apologize for lecturing you so much lately. About Isaac. You know I'll always worry about you, but watching you in there tonight, I realized that you do look happier than you have in a long time. More…you. So I'm going to stop nagging and start cheering you on instead. You deserve a good man, Delaney, and I'm hoping that's what this guy turns out to be."

"Aw, thanks, Sis. But you talking like that sounds like I'm about to fulfill Nan's tarot card prediction and elope."

She laughed while Mia smiled uncomfortably.

"It's a joke, Mi. I'm not going anywhere, you know that." Del looked toward the lamplights glowing softly over Main Street. "As for Isaac, right now he's just fun to be around. Will it last? Who knows. But for the first time in forever, instead of wanting to run away, I'm content to take things one day at a time and see what happens."

A gentle smile lit her sister's face. "That's my girl. Now, get out of here. I'm sure you have some web stuff to share."

"Something like that." Del winked, then waved her sister good-bye. Window rolled up and defenses down, she finished her text to Isaac with a smile.

I'll share more tomorrow, can't wait to see you.

Chapter Ten

ISAAC SPENT FRIDAY cleaning and primping—neither of which he planned to admit to anyone. Since he was about to have the first company he'd had since moving in, though, both tasks were necessary. He even bathed Louie—something neither of them enjoyed. But he'd be darned if everything wasn't perfect for their first date.

Well, as perfect as a first date could be, considering he was in an outdated rental property with minimal furnishings and having his date bring carryout so he could avoid being spotted in public. Not ideal, but tonight he didn't care about any of that. It was Delaney he looked forward to being with, not stuff or crowds.

Yes, Will had warned him to stay the course, but Delaney was like sunshine to his formerly overcast existence. After the year he'd had so far, being around someone who could lift his spirits was quickly becoming a hard habit to break.

Isaac spied her truck rolling up the drive shortly before seven and hurried outside to help her bring dinner in.

"Hey there, beautiful," he said, giving her a quick kiss as

she stepped from the truck. His compliment was sincere—she was rocking that pair of cutoff jeans and a pink, off-the-shoulder tee. Del had on her favorite sandals again, too, showing off painted toes that matched her top.

"Aw, thank you, handsome. I sure hope you're hungry—you ordered a ton of food."

He pulled her closer and nuzzled the hollow beneath her ear. "Sure am."

She shivered in his arms, the reaction giving him confidence. His lips traveled north, grazing the shell of her ear. "*Starving*."

Del drew in a quick breath, her hands tightening their grip on his hips. She turned her face toward his and whispered, "That makes two of us. Now help me get the food inside before you see my hangry side."

She gave his lips a playful nip, then pushed him away on a laugh. Though the last thing he wanted to do was let go, Isaac wasn't sure he was ready to tangle with her hangry side. So instead, he stayed back to receive the items she withdrew from her truck's cab: one large pizza box, a full plastic carryout bag, and a twelve pack of Landshark.

He looked from the beverages to Delaney, who offered him a shrug and coy smile.

"It's part of my usual Friday routine," she said. "There's fresh limes in the bag, too."

Isaac nearly dropped to one knee. Where had this woman been his whole life?

The pizza turned out to be amazing, the cheesy garlic bread divine, and the beers smooth and cold. But it was the company he enjoyed most. Louie was thrilled to have her here, too; he hadn't let Del get more than half a rump away from him since her arrival.

"You ready to see the progress I've made on the website?" he asked after they'd polished off the last of the garlic bread.

"Nah, I think we've both worked hard this week and deserve a break for tonight. Besides, we've got all weekend."

All weekend. Isaac liked the sound of that. His gaze shifted to her lips. "Did you have something else in mind?"

"Mmm-hmm." She drained the last of her beer and reached for a second. "I wanna go outside and catch the sunset with you and Louie."

Isaac shrugged and drained his drink as well. "Sounds good to me. Best view of that is in the backyard."

Restocked on beverages, the trio headed out the back door. Isaac had ordered two lounge chairs for the back deck shortly after he'd moved in—one for him and one for Louie. As soon as his dog was snapped to his long, backyard lead, he dutifully hopped into his usual seat, leaving Del and Isaac looking at the remaining chair.

"Guess we're going to have to Roshambo for it," she said on a laugh.

"Nah, I think we can both fit." He sat sideways, as far up on the seat as he could and patted the remaining space beside him. "See? Plenty of room for you here."

"But we can't see the sunset if we're facing that way," she said, turning him to sit facing forward. He let his legs hang over each side, and she settled gently into the space between, her soft perfume washing over him. Isaac wrapped his free arm around her, guiding her back until she was resting against his chest. A contented sigh escaped her.

"Comfy?" he asked.

"Very," she said. "I might have to take you home and add you to my living room collection."

"Not sure that'd be in your best interest," he teased. "Your grocery bill would climb significantly."

"I believe that, after watching all the carbs you just put away," she said on a laugh. "But can you cook?"

He took a drink of his beer, then shrugged. "I've got a few go-to dishes that aren't too shabby."

"Well, then you'd do much better than my davenport. It's absolutely worthless in the kitchen."

They shared a laugh, then fell into a comfortable silence. She felt so perfect, resting on his chest. Though it was still warm outside, a nice breeze helped to keep the night's humidity—and mosquitoes—at bay. As the sun sank closer to the horizon, Isaac silently wished it would slow its descent.

"Isaac, can I ask you something?"

He tensed at the unexpected question. "Sure."

She remained relaxed against him, her face toward the sun. "You're not really a hermit, are you?"

He smirked. "Not by nature, no."

"But something happened, didn't it? Something that made you want to hide away from the world for a while?"

So perceptive and so deadly accurate. When would this woman stop surprising him? "Yes," he admitted, resisting the urge to lie, and silently wishing that would satisfy her curiosity.

"Was it something illegal?"

"No," he said, grinning.

"Running from an estranged wife?"

At that, he laughed. "No."

"An estranged fiancée?"

"Definitely not." *Thank the heavens for that.*

Del took a long drink from her beer, then set the empty bottle down. Isaac braced himself for what she was preparing to ask him next.

"What made you want to stop?"

He frowned. "Made me want to stop what?"

"Being a hermit, staying tucked away from everyone."

She turned her face toward his, brows drawn together. Isaac felt himself drowning in her clear blue eyes. He gripped his beer tighter as the truth escaped him on a whisper. "You."

Del's eyes widened, and Isaac feared for a moment she might bolt. Instead, she swiveled to sit facing him, drawing his forehead to hers.

"If you're not ready for this, for me, I'll understand."

He set his beer to the side and traced a thumb across her

cheek, thanking the stars above for sending him such an amazing, selfless soul. "I'm not sure what I'm ready for, but it's definitely not you leaving."

A faint smile tugged at her lips. "Fair enough. The night's still young."

"Is it?"

He kissed her softly, tasting the beer on her lips. She kissed him back softly…then nipped his lower lip. She arched one brow, a mischievous look in her eyes. "Definitely."

Gone were the soft, tentative kisses, now replaced by hungry, need-filled, possessive ones. Isaac pulled her into his lap, wanting her closer, needing to feel her, to taste her. His lips left hers to trace a trail along her jawline, down her neck, and across her bare shoulder. Del curled her fingers into his hair and whispered his name, the sound spurring him on. He traced the hem of her shirt, his fingers finding the smooth skin beneath. She pulled his mouth back to hers, kissing him soundly, deeply. A soft hiss escaped her as his hands slid higher, brushing the underside of her breasts.

Isaac paused, waiting for a sign of permission. Del broke their kiss and shifted above him, her lips creating their own trail along his stubbly jawline and up to his earlobe.

"You keep this up, and I won't be able to tell you to stop."

His fingers skimmed higher, over a lacy bra to brush across her sensitive nub. "Like this?"

"Yes," she breathed, eyes closed and arching into him. "Just like that."

He slipped his thumb under her bra and continued to tease her taut peaks, taking great pleasure in watching the confident Delaney Brooks squirm.

"Please tell me you have something."

He looked to the sky, grateful that he'd humored his favorite grocery store cashier who'd seen him talking to Del the other week and insisted he be prepared "just in case."

"I do," he said, tugging her shirt aside to suckle one nipple, then the other. A needy mew escaped her. "Think a box of three will be enough?"

"For now."

Del shifted above him, her hand tracing down his chest to the bulge in his shorts. She caressed it through the fabric, and Isaac nearly came undone. Enough with the petting—he wanted more.

In one swift motion, Isaac shifted from under Del and reached to unclip Louie from his lead. "Time for bed," he said, signing as he went. The second Louie was safely inside, Isaac doubled back, picked Del up, and tossed her over his shoulder.

"Wait!" she cried, with a laugh. "Our bottles!"

"Woman, I've been waiting for this moment since I met you," he said, angling for the door. "Those bottles can wait."

DEL AWOKE TRAPPED inside a cocoon, darkness and warmth all around her. After a moment of panic, soft snoring reminded her of where she was—in Isaac's bed, curled naked against him under the sheets, and sandwiched there by one overweight bulldog lying atop the sheets on her other side. She turned her head to find Louie sleeping like a people, his head on the pillow that had been intended for her. Or maybe that was his usual sleeping space, and here she was, invading it.

She snuggled closer to Isaac's long, lean body, enjoying that he didn't seem to mind, and let the memories of the night wash over her. Of Isaac's kisses, of his touch. Of the way he'd so thoughtfully—and thoroughly—focused on her needs. It'd been a while since she'd been with anyone, so her first orgasm had come hot and fast. Number two had waited for Isaac. Number three was what had landed her here, sleepy, sated, and in utter bliss.

Why on earth had she gone so long without sex?

Because there hadn't been anyone who'd caught her eye like Isaac in years. And not just his looks but his kindness and generosity. Although, she'd be lying if she didn't admit to being drawn to his sexy smile and that delicious stubble she loved to rake her fingers through.

Love—now there was a word she'd better be careful to not start using. Tonight had been fun, but it'd also been all about lust; she was smart enough to know they were not one and the same. Yes, she genuinely enjoyed his company and had no intentions to stop seeing him anytime soon, but they'd only known each other a short time. It was far too early to be throwing out the *L* word.

It was not, however, too early to be labeled as the clingy type, something she was not.

"I've got to get home," she whispered to her handsome hermit.

On a frown and with eyes still closed he mumbled, "No, stay."

She shifted to stroke his stubbly cheek. She hated to go, but it was necessary. Small towns talked, and she wasn't sure she was ready to make the headlines. Also, the clothes she brought with her would never do for their planned landscaping activities after sunup. "Can't. But I'll be back soon."

"Promise?" he asked, still more asleep than not.

"Yes." She placed a soft kiss on his cheek.

He mumbled something else, then rolled to his side. Del waited for his breathing to smooth into a slow cadence, then slipped silently from the bed. Louie opened one eye at her stirring but didn't bother moving a muscle, allowing her to collect her clothes, still scattered about the floor, and trod off to find the hallway bathroom. Having dressed and quietly freshened up, she eased out the front door and found her way home.

Three a.m.

She grinned at the time displayed on her dash. Driving home was much preferable to her earlier years doing the "walk of shame" trek across campus. Though, for her, sex hadn't ever been something she'd felt ashamed about; tonight was no different. Had it not been so late, she might have even given it one more try before heading out. But morning would come early for them both, and they had a full day of yardwork ahead of them.

Though, with as much time as he'd spent on her website this week, she planned to do the lion's share of yardwork today. And to prevent him from objecting, she'd be getting there at nine instead of ten like she'd told him over dinner, to get a head start on their work. The forecast had called for a warm but clear day, and she planned to make the most of it. Who knew how many more days like this Indiana would offer?

Plans for the day were still running circles in her mind when Del made it home, peeled off her clothes—again—and crawled into bed. Asleep the minute her head hit the pillow, she awakened a short time later by the sound of a text alert from her phone. She cracked one eye open and was shocked to find her room filled with muted sunlight. A quick glance at her phone found it was already eight o'clock.

Eight o'clock?!

Darn it, she'd forgotten to set her alarm. Thank goodness for the text or she'd never have made it back to Isaac's by nine. A few swipes and she opened the new message from Margaret Harper.

Got in a little late last night, didn't we?

Del grimaced. Such was life, living next to watchful insomniacs. “We don’t need to share that with anyone else,” she texted back.

Margaret sent a little smiling devil emoji.

Your secret’s safe with me. Hope you two had LOTS of fun.

Del sat up on a groan, resisting the urge to text back and dig this hole any deeper. Of course Margaret would connect the dots so quickly. Also, Del knew better than to believe their little “secret” was truly safe—that would only happen until Margaret’s sisters woke up. All she could hope was that they would keep it among themselves long enough to give her time to tell Mia.

Which, she decided while in the shower, was going to have to wait. Not because she was hiding anything from her older sister, she simply didn’t have the time right now. Mia had always loved her sleep and wouldn’t be up for at least another hour or two. By then, Del would be well into her work at Isaac’s.

Besides, she was going to need to tell Mia—who else could help her craft the best introduction of Isaac to their father? Because hermit or not, if this thing continued between them, Stephen Brooks was going to insist on meeting him. There was no guarantee the two men would hit it off, since her father had been called curmudgeonly a time or two, but—

Whoa.

Was she really having this conversation with herself? Introducing Isaac to the family?

Del shook her head and finished getting ready for a day of playing in the dirt. Time to curb that line of thought. Just because they'd shared an amazing night together didn't mean she was allowed to go and get all hung up on the guy, especially when she still didn't know his whole story. And was what he had shared with her even the truth?

Crap. There was another line of thought that needed stopped. Why were old habits so hard to break? She paused before her bedroom mirror and leveled a stern look at herself.

"Isaac is not Jonathan," she told her reflection. "He said there was no other woman, and you need to believe him until he gives you reason not to. He'll share his story when he's ready."

Her reflection gave it some thought, then nodded in agreement. Del just hoped the rest of the story would come soon so she could put these worries to rest. Until then, she just had to trust him.

Hopefully, this time, her plan wouldn't come back to bite her.

Not that she had time to sit around and worry about it. This week, the bookstore fundraiser group would have its hands full, their planning kicking into full swing. There were sponsors to procure and advertising to price out and prep ahead of the event, and food and drink vendors to line up for the day of. And ticket sales. And parking strategies to iron out. And press releases to send out. And—

Del shook her head. No sense in getting overwhelmed about it. They had an awesome planning committee team assembled, and she needed to trust the process. Besides, worrying or not, it wouldn't all be done today. There were too many pieces in motion, too many steps yet to be determined. One of her father's often-used phrases of wisdom came to mind:

How do you eat an elephant? One bite at a time.

That's what this fundraiser was: a giant, bookstore-sized elephant. She'd tackled mammoth projects before, and with the help of her friends and family, she would do it again. Only this time, she also had one handsome hermit to not only help but also provide delicious distractions as needed.

Thank heavens for that, because looking to the weeks ahead, she was going to need a fair number of distractions to keep her sanity in check. And she couldn't think of anyone she'd rather be distracted by right now than him.

Chapter Eleven

ISAAC WOKE MONDAY morning, actually excited for the day to begin. Usually, Mondays were at the bottom of his favorites list—the past seven months, even more so. But that was before he'd let Del into his life. Now he was pumped to start a new week, and curious to see what each day would bring.

With Delaney, he never knew what to expect.

Friday night had been the highlight of his year, starting out with great food and excellent company. But once they'd hit the bedroom? It'd been fireworks from the first touch. She'd been insatiable, eager to please, and open to being pleased. Usually, his "first" nights were filled with tentative moves and a good share of fumbling.

Not with Del. He'd thought she was amazing before, but Friday night had taken that appreciation to a whole new level. Throughout the weekend, they'd each found ways to lure one another back to his bed. He couldn't get enough of her and doubted he ever would.

With that realization came another first: actually dreading the day he would have to leave Bourbon Falls.

Isaac brushed the thought aside, unwilling to let anything dampen his spirits. He and Del were having fun, not preparing wedding vows. Who knew? Maybe they'd get sick of one another before Will got his damage control strategy to work. Until then, Isaac was going to savor every day he had with Del, so long as she would have him.

He texted her midmorning, after breezing his way through M&M's online meeting, unable to think of much else.

Care to join me for lunch? Caesar Salad topped with grilled chicken.

Her response came within seconds.

Would love to! I'll swing by after Chase is back from his.

Excellent, that would give him a few more minutes to prepare.

Perfect. And lunch comes with a show. Prepare to be amazed.

This time, her response took a few more seconds to arrive.

Um, I don't think I have that long of a lunch…

Isaac laughed aloud.

The website, Del. I was talking about the website. LOL

Del sent back a blushing emoji, then let him know she'd text when she was on her way. Unfortunately, now he was thinking about all the delicious things he could do to her if neither of them did have to work this afternoon. But there was always tonight. Hopefully, she didn't already have plans.

He refocused on his laptop, diving back into the proposal specs he was working his way through. Though stretched thin, Will had still managed to get his foot in the door with three excellent potential clients, albeit slightly outside their usual target market. Hopefully, between their team's perseverance and the dying social media dumpster fire, business would begin to grow again. The East Coast was a hot market right now, and he knew some of their newest software solutions could easily be cloned and customized to benefit other future clients.

By the time Del texted that she was on her way, Isaac had become completely submersed in his work. In a panic, he bolted from the room to throw together their lunch. She walked in a few minutes later and bent to calm a whining Louie, eyeing the kitchen now in disarray.

"I take it someone got lost in their work after we texted?" she asked, a knowing look in her eye.

"Maybe," he said with a wink.

"How about I take poor Louie to his bathroom in the yard and give you another minute to get everything together?"

Isaac stepped around the counter and pulled her into a long kiss. She tasted as sweet as ever, her lips soft against his. He had to remind himself to let go, that they were both technically on the clock. On a grin, he returned to his food preparation tasks. "Thank you."

"Thank *you*."

She waggled her brows then disappeared outside with Louie. Isaac was just dishing up their salads when his cell phone began to ring. Will's name scrolled across its screen.

"Not a good time," Isaac murmured, silencing the ring.

Will called right back.

"Dammit." Isaac snatched up his cell and shot a quick text to his partner, asking what was up.

Can you talk?

Isaac glanced out the front window to where Del stood, coaxing Louie to hurry up and do his thing.

No. What's up?

Have a bid question for you, call when you aren't in the john.

Isaac responded that he would, relieved Will hadn't insisted he call right then. But now he was curious as to what the update was about. Was the media storm closer to ending, or had more thunder rolled in?

The front door squeaked open, followed by doggie nails clicking on the entryway tile.

"Man, there is no hurrying this dog to do anything, is there?"

Isaac pushed his thoughts about Will and Katrina aside on a grin. "Welcome to my world."

"It's a good thing you're cute, buddy." Del gave Louie a scratch behind the ears then unclipped his lead and hung it by the door. "Still need some help in here?"

"Nope, have a seat. I just need to grab my laptop. I know you're short on time, figured I could give you the grand tour while we eat."

Isaac grabbed his cell phone from the counter and made for his office. The last thing he needed was Will to change his mind and call back and Del to try to be helpful by answering. Though he was starting to hate feeling like he was sneaking around behind Will's back. Which, honestly, he was. He just wished there was a way to tell Will about her without him freaking out. Because knowing William McManus, that's exactly what he would do.

"Okay, this isn't a hundred percent done," he warned as he set the machine down on the end of the counter, "but it's close. I took in your suggestions from last week and added a few more pictures of downtown over here. Visitors click on this, and it takes them to the registration page. All I need is for you to get the banking information from Faye, and that part will be ready to test. Oh, and I added a link to your town's website and added a map that automatically shows all the store names and locations so people can explore all of Bourbon Falls while they're here."

Del was surprisingly quiet.

"What's wrong?"

"Nothing." Her eyes began to glisten. "It's…perfect."

Isaac took one of her hands in his and gave it a gentle squeeze. "I'm glad you like it. Do you think the others will, too?"

"Are you kidding me?" She laughed, fanning the unshed tears from her eyes. "They're gonna absolutely flip out when they see this. When can I show it to them?"

"When's your next meeting?"

"Tomorrow evening."

Isaac nodded. "Here, I'll send you a link to the test site. Since the money piece isn't done, you all can play around in it without hurting anything. I'll just clear it all out before we go live."

"Wow. I can't believe we're nearly there. And you!" Del leaned over to pull him into a bear hug. "None of this would even be possible without all you've done!"

Isaac wrapped his arms around her. "Don't give me too much credit, now. I'm not the only person who can put together a simple website."

"Okay, first, it's not simple. And second"—she leveled a stern look at him—"stop being so damned modest. This looks amazing, and the whole town will soon be in your debt."

"In my debt, hmm?" He leaned in and nuzzled the soft spot beneath her ear. "Does that mean I get to choose the preferred method of repayment?"

"Sorry, buster, we already worked out those terms. Landscaping for website, remember?"

He nibbled her earlobe and felt her shiver in his arms. "But I added that cool map. Surely, that's got to be worth something."

Isaac was teasing, of course. Adding a Google map took virtually no time at all.

"Hmm, that is a good point," she said, brushing her lips across his in a slow tease. "Perhaps we'll have to discuss this further over dinner on Wednesday."

"Wednesday? Why not tonight?"

She drew back, lips pursed in a disappointed pout. "Sorry, Isaac. I promised Aunt Faye I'd cover for her at the bookstore tonight so she could go talk to her banking buddy. Of course, you're always welcome to pop by and keep me company."

"I can't. Brooklyn wasn't free to cover for her?"

"No, she's got marching band practice, and Mia is apparently on band mom duty tonight, making sure no one passes out from the heat or whatever."

"Bummer." He gave her a peck on the cheek and drew back, trying to keep the disappointment from showing on his face. "But I'm sure Faye appreciates the help."

"She does, and I'm happy to do it. Of course, it probably won't be as fun as if I were over here with you two studs, but I'll make the most of it." She winked, then glanced out the window. "Plus, it's supposed to rain tonight, so I'd rather it be me there than little B, in case the leak starts again. Hopefully, the tarp will stay in place. If not, you know where I'll be."

"Just be safe," he cautioned. "I'd hate for you to slip and the bookstore become haunted."

"You never know, it might help boost business."

She flashed him a smile, then dug into her salad. All too soon she was heading back to work, and Isaac was left to his own devices once more. From his kitchen window, he watched darker clouds roll in, and the good mood he'd started the day with began to wane.

While he'd like to think this thing with Del was a simple case of infatuation or the excitement that often came with new relationships, he had a sneaking suspicion it was developing into more than that. He loved when she was here and hated when she was gone. And though she'd been a good sport so far with his peculiar, hermit-like ways, a vibrant woman like Del could never fall for a man reluctant to leave home.

Isaac watched the clouds swirling overhead, jealous of their freedom to ebb and flow. He missed coming and going as he pleased, missed living his own life the way he wanted. As he stood scowling out the window over his sink, his phone buzzed with a new text message from Will.

You free yet?

Not hardly, Isaac thought with a snort. He turned from the window, his gaze landing on the car keys dangling from a hook across the room. Keys that, until now, he'd only allowed himself to use for late-night grocery trips. Maybe it was time to change that up a bit, be the outgoing type of man Del deserved to be with. After all, happy employees *were* the most productive…

DEL SAT BEHIND the cash register at Brooks Books that night, perched on Faye's beloved barstool, gaze roving between the leak-prone corner of the room and the weather radar on her cell phone. So far, there'd been no signs of water inside, despite the heavier-than-expected rain outside. She knew she ought to trust the repairman who'd put the tarp down a few weeks back, but it was hard to do, listening to the wind whistle through the street signs outside.

They couldn't get this talent show booked and over with fast enough.

She reached for the store computer and pulled up Isaac's test website, still in awe of his creation. Though she didn't get online much, Del could still recognize quality when she saw it. The design was beautiful, the clickable links intuitive and easy to find. But it was the tone that made all the difference to her—country but not overly so, small town but not hick. That he'd thought to include that map with their town's shop names and even an option to view at a street-view level touched her heart. He may not be a native of Bourbon Falls, but he seemed to truly care about its future.

Would he stay here long term? Is that why he had agreed to help save the bookstore? Surely, he hadn't done all this work just to get his landscaping done. If so, he'd gotten the raw end of the deal. They were nearly done with the landscaping already, only needing to put down stone and mulch. She could only imagine how many hours he'd spent on the website design.

Then again, he did seem to love doing it. She remembered the sparkle in his eyes as he shared the prototype with her at lunch, the excitement in his voice. It was the same kind of reaction she had when sharing landscape designs with her clients, her passion for the work bubbling to the surface. Maybe that's why their relationship felt so easy—they were both passionate about their crafts. Because it sure felt easy. Maybe even too easy at times.

Especially at his place, in his arms. In his bed…

The bell over the front door jingled, startling Del. She looked to the entrance, where her newcomer was fumbling to close their umbrella.

"Evening, thanks for stopping by."

"Busy night?" was the muffled response.

"Hardly. You're the only one who's ventured in tonight."

"That's what I was hoping for."

Del's heartbeat quickened. "Isaac?"

He lowered his umbrella and flashed her a smile. "Hey, there, beautiful."

"Wow, I…I can't believe you're here." She rounded the counter then paused. "You're not going to spontaneously combust or anything, are you? You know, being this far from home and all?"

He laughed, one of her new favorite sounds filling one of her absolute favorite places.

"I sure hope not," he said, leaning his umbrella near the door. "Especially before I've had the chance to receive the grand tour."

"That's very sweet, but you don't have to say that. I

know bookstores aren't everyone's cup of tea."

"Not gonna lie, it's been a while since I've been in an actual bookstore, and nothing like this. Also? Your aunt needs to update her website, because it's not doing her shop justice. This place is really cool."

She looked around the space, trying to see it the way he did. Having grown up in Brooks Books, she'd explored every nook and cranny of the store over the years, from its rustic brick walls to the hand-built islands of shelves and the storefront displays. "You really think so?"

"Definitely. I've looked at a lot of independent bookstores online the past few weeks, trying to get ideas for how to best feature yours on our event page. This store has such a warm and inviting feel to it. Makes you want to come in and stay awhile."

Del smiled. "That's exactly what my mother always wanted—a welcoming space to help foster the love of reading. It's why we still host story time for toddlers and young readers every other Wednesday evening. Not sure if I've told you this, but it's my favorite time of the week."

He studied her for a minute, head tipped to one side. "I didn't realize you had such a heart for kids."

"Oh, I love kids—love to get them all riled up and send them on their way." She laughed. "I've had plenty of practice at it, too, with Brooklyn. But I knew she wouldn't be little forever, so this gets me my little kid fix each week. And it's the best feeling when you have a group that's totally into the story and hanging on your every word—like watching their love of reading blossom right before your eyes."

Isaac wandered toward the back of the store, Del following to offer commentary where needed. "But you don't just sell kid books, I see."

"Nope. We've got a little of everything, really. New books and old. Faye thought it would encourage people to read more if we gave them an option to sell us the books back when they were done. Since there's no library in Bourbon Falls, she thought this was the next best thing. Of course, she doesn't make anything off the used books, but that's never been the store's main focus."

"And here?" he asked, stepping around the far shelving unit and kneeling to look on its lowest shelf. "What's waiting in the shadows here?"

"Back here?"

As she bent to get a better look at the section he was motioning toward, Isaac tugged her face to his and gave her a long, slow kiss.

"Sorry," he grinned, tracing her jawline with his thumb. "Been wanting to do that since you left."

"I'll allow it, but just this once," she said with a wink. "Got a whole town watching through those front windows, so we can't stay here long."

"Ah, yes. I should have known that." He stood and moseyed on, turning his back to the front window with a conspiratorial grin. "First time I've kissed anyone in a bookstore, for the record."

"First time I've been kissed in here and not duked the guy responsible," she answered.

"What!"

Del laughed. "Herbie Meyers snuck in and planted one on me in the fourth grade. He left with a fat lip. Pretty sure I got grounded for that one."

"Definitely not good business to go punching your customers."

She scoffed. "Not good manners to be making moves on the staff, either."

"Touché." Isaac motioned toward a newer rocking chair and woven rug in the young reader's section. "And I take it this is where the magic happens?"

"It is."

"Are there pictures of this anywhere? Because it would be the perfect addition to our 'why you should support our fundraiser' page."

"I'm sure there are, but they're probably not all that recent. Maybe I can hit Mia up to take some pictures next time."

"Hit me up for what?"

Isaac froze as Mia's voice rang out from the back hall, genuine fear in his eyes. Something in his past certainly had him spooked. Del hated to see him this way; hated the thought of him leaving even more.

"Stay here," she whispered. "I'll be right back."

He met her gaze for a moment, hesitating, then nodded and angled for the farthest shelves from the checkout counter. Del grabbed a few books to make it look like she'd been busy reshelving them and made her way toward the front of the store. Mild panic set in when she spied both Mia and Brooklyn lingering at the checkout counter.

Alone, Mia wouldn't have been a problem; she'd never seen Isaac before and wouldn't know him from a stranger. Brooklyn, however, had. Del walked past them, drawing their attention toward her and away from her lone customer.

"Hit you up for some fall coupons," she said with a wink. "And what are you doing here on your night off? I thought you guys had some band thing going on."

Brooklyn hitched a thumb toward the front windows. "In case you hadn't noticed, it's kinda pouring outside."

"So? You can't march in the rain?"

Brooklyn rolled her eyes.

"Rain, yes. Downpour? Not so much, so they let the kids go early." Mia shrugged. "They got no complaints from either of us."

Del laughed. "I can see that. So, what, you came in here to relieve me so I can go home early?"

"No way," Brooklyn cried. "I already have to work tomorrow, so you guys can have another one of your planning meetings."

Del stuck her tongue out at Brooklyn, who did the same in return as she headed for the YA section. A quick glance confirmed that Isaac was still "shopping" in the back corner of the store. How long would he linger before giving up and sneaking out?

"That's actually why we stopped by," Mia said, stepping forward to extract a notebook from her oversized purse. "I had an idea for the talent show that I wanted to run by you before the meeting. With there being prize money involved, I thought that instead of us choosing a winner, we should do something a little different."

"Like?"

"What if we let the crowd decide the winner? Let everyone vote and then have someone tally it up. Brooklyn said there's a kid in her class who knows how to make phone apps. If he could make one for us, it'd be even more like those TV talent shows, and might draw a bigger crowd."

Del caught movement out of the corner of her eye. Brooklyn was moving away from the door, Isaac moving closer to it. Maybe it was best to keep Mia talking so he could slip out; she could always stop by his place later. "But not everyone is techie like you guys."

"Ugh, Aunt *Del*..."

"What? I'm not the only one who can't figure stuff like that out. *Go* figure."

Mia gave her a weird look, but the message had been received; Isaac crept closer to the door. Brooklyn had picked up the latest book in a series she followed, keeping her back to him.

"Well," Mia said, tapping her pen to the notepad. "What if we had volunteers in the crowd who can collect votes for the less capable?"

"That might work, maybe even have them dressed in neon colors so they're easy to find." Del moved over a few steps to keep her sister facing away from the door. Isaac had reached the last section of shelving. If he kept his head down, they might not even notice him slip out. She willed him to hurry up and make his move.

That's when she got the start of a tickle in her nose.

"Of course, if we don't get enough people to sign up for the event, this is all a moot point," Mia said with a sigh, still oblivious to the chess match going on in the store. "But I think the town would be that much more engaged if we included them in the decision process, don't you?"

"Instead of have it be a surprise?" Del pushed her tongue against the roof of her mouth, fighting the oncoming sneeze. "Yeah, I guess it could—*achoo*!"

"Bless you," responded three voices.

Del held her breath. Mia didn't react, her attention still focused on the notepad. A subtle glance out across the store found Isaac reaching for his umbrella…but now Brooklyn was MIA.

Where the heck had her niece wandered off to?

As Isaac's umbrella's fabric slid against the brick's rough surface, Del spied her niece coming around the other side of the mystery section. *Don't look up, please, don't look—*

"Oh," Brooklyn said from across the room. "Hey, Isaac."

Up.

Isaac lowered his umbrella, a sheepish grin on his face. "Heya, Brooklyn. Ladies."

"So you're the infamous Isaac Manning." Mia started forward before Del could catch her. She followed close behind, grimacing. "I never got the chance to properly thank you for helping rescue my daughter. Or apologize for her wrecking your yard."

"I was just glad she wasn't hurt."

Isaac remained in place, feet glued to the floor. And while Mia might not have heard the rising anxiety in his voice, Del picked up on it right away.

"Uh, yeah, so Mia, Isaac. Isaac, Mia." She stepped between them. "Anyway, Isaac, we won't hold you up. I know you've got a ton of work to catch up on since you've spent so much time on our *website*. Ladies, tell the nice man goodbye."

"Bye, Isaac," Brooklyn called over her shoulder, her attention already having shifted to another book.

"Yes, thank you again for all your work on the website," Mia said, now studying him intently.

He offered an awkward nod, then hurried from the store like a spooked rabbit. But why?

"You're right, he's definitely handsome," Mia murmured, watching through narrowed eyes as he dashed through the rain to his vehicle parked outside. "But is he always so jumpy?"

Only when he's out in public. "I'm sure he's just got a lot on his mind."

What it was, exactly, Del was dying to know.

Chapter Twelve

ISAAC DROVE NORTH out of town Tuesday after Del finished with her fundraiser planning meeting, her in his passenger seat and Louie in between them, stretching from the backseat to plant his front feet on the center console. It was the first time they'd driven with a passenger in the front seat, but thankfully his bully was taking it in stride. Louie loved car rides. Tonight, as they headed out of town to some hole-in-the-wall—and hopefully mostly deserted—ice cream stand Del knew about a few towns over, Louie stood between them, not a care in the world.

And Isaac was jealous as hell.

"You're still worrying."

He glanced over the top of Louie's head to Del, who was watching him with one brow raised. Barely three weeks he'd known the woman and already she was starting to read him like a book.

"Maybe a little."

He played the fib off as casually as he could, struggling to keep his anxiety in check as he turned his attention back to the road. He'd taken a big risk, going to visit Del at the bookstore yesterday. Had been foolishly overconfident that no one else would be out on a night like that. Now here he sat, mind racing and paranoia running rampant.

Why? Because the look on Del's sister's face had said it all: *I feel like I know you from somewhere.*

Had it been anyone else, anyone at all, he could have pretended to be a stranger just passing through. But no, it had to be Brooklyn who showed up with Mia last night, the only person in Bourbon Falls beside Del who'd seen him without a disguise on since he'd arrived to town. Though, it wasn't her fault that she'd seen him—he was the idiot who'd blurted out "bless you" on autopilot. If he'd kept his mouth shut, he could have slipped out the door without anyone noticing and wouldn't be in his current mess.

Strike that. If he'd stayed home, he wouldn't be in this mess. No, even that wasn't quite right. If he hadn't dated Katrina, he wouldn't be in this predicament.

Even that was technically still his fault. She'd been cute, and her offer to do coffee had given his ego a surprise stroke. Before her, it'd been a while since he'd allowed himself time to date. He and Will had spent years getting their business off the ground, and while Will was always good at striking the right balance between work and home life, Isaac had the tendency to focus too much on work and not enough on home—something his post-college girlfriends hadn't appreciated.

But it wasn't until Del came along that he wanted to step

away from his keyboard and enjoy life. Ironic, as this was also the time in his life he was supposed to be laying low. Yes, he'd been lonely when she first arrived on the scene, but she was smart and funny and confident and caring and selfless. With so many admirable traits, how could he not want to spend time with this woman?

Working with her these past few weekends on his landscaping, he'd seen a passion in her eyes for earth and design. At the bookstore, he'd seen another side of Delaney Brooks, one that showed a passion for her family and her community. And while that was an honor to experience in and of itself, it was her surprise and delight at his arrival that'd washed away all his apprehensions about leaving home. In that moment, he believed he'd do it again every night to get that response from her.

Then Mia happened, and now he was recanting that idea.

He couldn't sneak into town every night to see Del, not without completely throwing caution to the wind. His skin was crawling with anxiety after only one person had seen his face and learned his identity. How bad would it be if there'd been more?

"I told you, you did great. Mia's always acted a little wary around new people until she gets to know them better. It's her inner mother thing."

Isaac nodded, wishing he could agree with Del's assessment. But Mia's wariness was warranted. If she had recognized him, she'd know his story. Irrational as it was, he kept waiting for her to arrive on his doorstep and call him out for living a lie. Or worse, show up at Del's and tell *her* that he was living a lie.

But he wasn't living a lie; he was just hiding here from his past, waiting for the dust to settle back east. It was shameful and embarrassing, but not technically a lie. Would Del see it the same way?

"If you say so," he said, forcing a smile.

She reached over and took his hand in hers. Great. Here she was, reassuring him when he wasn't being entirely forthcoming with her. He rubbed his thumb across the back of her fingers, torn. Should he tell her the whole story or keep it safely buried like he and Will had agreed he would?

I should tell her. Confidence in the decision washed over him. As supportive as Del had been since first they'd met, she out of everyone would understand.

"You know, there is—"

Del's phone started playing James Taylor's "Fire and Rain," and he felt her hand leave his.

"Sorry, I should get this," she whispered. "Heya, Pops. What's up?"

Isaac held his breath. This was it, the cease-and-desist call from her father, ordering her to stop seeing him after Mia put two and two together. Isaac drove on, waiting for the other shoe to drop.

"Aw, man, sorry to hear that about poor Rex. Sure, that's

no problem at all. I'll pop over a few times tomorrow while you're at work to make sure he's doing okay."

Isaac held his breath while she chatted a moment more, then exchanged good-byes with her father. "Everything okay?"

She offered him a small smile. "Oh, yeah. My father's dog is just getting older and has seizures every now and then. Vet doesn't seem too worried about it so long as they are few and far between, I guess. Pops will be at the station tomorrow, so I need to stop over a few times and make sure Rex is doing all right."

Relief washed over him; no second shoe yet. "Ah, I see. How old is he?"

"My dad? Fifty-six, though I swear the man thinks he's in his twenties some days."

Isaac chuckled. "I meant Rex."

"Oh." Del laughed. "We're not really sure. He was a rescue dog like Louie."

"Man, I hope he'll be okay."

"Me too. Rex has been a great dog, having him around has helped Pops a lot."

"Oh?"

Del kept her gaze forward, her voice taking on a softer tone. "My youngest sister, Hannah, skipped town after high school. No one knows why, but I always kinda thought she might. Hannah Banana never really fit in here. Always had her head in the clouds and got picked on a lot. Chase, he loved her from the day they met and made it his personal mission to protect her from the jerks and bullies."

"Just Chase?"

She flashed him a mischievous smile. "Oh, I may have kicked a few butts, too, over the years. Gotta take care of your own, you know?"

He didn't know. His parents had always been distracted by life, his sister in her own little world. Their chemistry was nothing like what he sensed Del shared with her family. It'd never bothered him, though, because he hadn't known any better. Hearing the adoration in Del's voice now, he found himself envious of what she'd grown up with. "I'm sure you took very good care of her."

"I did." She dipped her head. "Hurt like hell when she left without saying good-bye."

Isaac reached for her hand. She let him take it, offering him a smile full of false bravado.

"I'm sure she had her reasons. But Pops, he took it the hardest. Aunt Faye brought Rex home a few weeks later—someone she knew was going into a nursing home and couldn't take him with her. My father had never been an animal person and wanted nothing to do with him at first; he was too busy sitting on the front porch each night, being mad at the world. Honestly, I think he sat out there so much that first summer holding out hope my sister would change her mind and come back home."

"I take it that didn't happen."

Del shook her head. "But ole Rex, he was bound and determined to worm his way into my father's heart. Each night, he'd go out and sit on the end of the porch while Pops glared at the front yard. And each night, Pops would ignore him, so the next night, Rex would scoot a little closer. By the end of week three, he was at Pops's side, and he's been there ever since." She sighed. "My old man still sits out on that porch most nights, watching and waiting."

"Do you think she'll ever come back?"

"I don't know. Aunt Faye insists she'll find her way home when she's ready, but only time will tell." Del shook her head. "Wow, sorry. Here I was trying to get you out for a fun evening and I went and got all serious on you."

"You talk about whatever you need to, Delaney. I'm happy to listen."

She gave his hand a squeeze then released it, smiles replacing the worry on her features once again. "Careful what you wish for, buddy."

His GPS guided them to turn into an empty parking lot small enough if he'd blinked, he would have missed it. Weeds grew waist-tall around the edges of the gravel surface, and a rundown camper trailer sat on blocks to one side. Isaac angled his vehicle into an imaginary parking space, in case anyone else showed up here tonight.

"Is this place even open?" he asked, eyeing the sliding window beneath a makeshift letterboard menu.

"Oh, yeah, the owner just always parks around back.

Come on, let's go get us some tasty treats."

She hopped out the passenger door without hesitation, motioning him to follow. He watched her round the engine. He'd follow this woman anywhere she led him. The thought should have scared him, but instead it brought him an unexpected peace.

Isaac beckoned his bully into the front seat and snapped the lead to Louie's collar. It was time to be honest with her, he decided, as they followed a broad-smiling Del to the order windows. No more secrets.

But how and when to have his tell-all moment?

"What do you have going on tomorrow night?" Del asked as their malts were being blended.

"Wild party at my place as always. You wanna crash it?" He waggled his brows.

"Sounds fun, but I have a better idea—since I need to go over to the farm to check on Rex for Pops, why don't we do a picnic dinner there? I can order carryout from the Sweet Mash, and make sure to get a double serving of cobbler this time. You can bring Louie along, and he and Rex can run around and play in the fenced area out back." The ice cream attendant handed a dog-sized vanilla cone out the window, which Del knelt to feed to Louie. "What do you think?"

Another evening with Del, his favorite dog, and his new favorite dessert sounded perfect. It'd also be the ideal time to tell her about the less-than-ideal cloud hanging over his head.

"I think it's a date."

DELANEY HELPED CHASE unload a truckload of fall flowers on Wednesday, grateful for the busy work. This late in the season, weekday residential shoppers were sporadic at best. And now that she and Isaac were starting to be a thing, she wished for the days to pass quickly so she could hurry up and get to her evenings with him.

Only, what she should be doing was throwing all her free time into the upcoming fundraiser.

She followed Chase with a tray of asters to the shop's front porch, shaking her head as she went. Who would have thought she of all people would go and find a boyfriend in the middle of a bookstore crisis? Though she couldn't feel too guilty about it. If she and Isaac hadn't hit it off, who knows if the website would have been finished so fast? Crazy as it sounded, Brooklyn sliding into his front yard had turned out to be a blessing in disguise for them all.

"So how many people do you all have signed up for this talent show of yours?" Chase asked, setting his tray next to the others they'd already unloaded.

"None yet. Just waiting on Faye to get her charity bank account stuff set up, then we'll cross our fingers and hope for a few brave souls to sign on."

He chuckled. "You don't sound very optimistic."

"Just don't want to get my hopes up too high, ya know?"

"Have faith, Del. The Sisters are all over this. If they say it'll work, it will work."

"I sure hope you're right. We can't lose the bookstore, Chase."

"Pfft, like the Brooks family would let that happen," he said with a wink. "But if you don't get enough entrants, I promise to convince the locals to sign up and fill the empty slots."

She pictured him, going door to door, drafting people, and couldn't help but laugh. "We need talent, Chase, not just bodies."

"Says who? Some of my favorite talent shows were the ones scarce on talent but full of heart."

Del planted a hand on one hip. "And just how many talent shows have you seen?"

"I don't know. How many did they make us suffer through in middle school?"

A devilish grin stole across his face, and Del swatted him with an empty cardboard box. "That doesn't count!"

"Just because you didn't win doesn't mean it didn't count!" he cried, shielding himself from her harmless attack. "Which reminds me, I've been meaning to ask—what's your act going to be?"

"My act?" She stopped swatting and stood there, momentarily speechless.

"Wait—you mean to tell me you haven't come up with an act yet?"

Del knelt to arrange the perennials closest to her. "I

hadn't event thought of it, to be honest. Haven't had time to."

"Of course not, you've been too busy helping that new man of yours design the website." Chase grabbed a few containers and placed them on his side of the porch. "So when do I get to meet this guy, anyway? Gotta make sure he's up to snuff, you know."

She rolled her eyes. "Whatever. You're just jealous because Mia got to meet him before you."

"Heck yeah, I'm jealous. Plus, I'm a better judge of character than she is. Less worried about everything."

Del offered him a fist bump. "Truth. For a while there, she was hounding me about being cautious around him. After meeting him the other night, though, she hasn't said a peep. Maybe seeing him with her own eyes helped her to realize how silly she was sounding."

"She worries because she cares, you know that."

"I do. But sometimes her paranoia starts to get contagious. I prefer to spend less time worrying and more time living."

"Well, I for one am hoping things between you and Isaac work out. You've got the Delaney glow back, and it looks damn good on you."

"Whatever."

"Whatever yourself. But if that guy even thinks about breaking your heart, he'd better look out."

Chase pounded a fist into his other hand, and Del shook

her head.

"Like you'd hurt anyone."

He shrugged. "I know people."

Which was true, he did know a few guys who wouldn't hesitate to talk sense into guys with their fists if they tried hurting her. They were all firefighters, and all worked under her father, the chief. Though Del would sooner take matters into her own hands than ask for any of their help, which they all knew.

"We're just having fun, Chase. It's way too early for hearts to get involved, much less broken." Before he could argue, she raised her hand and continued, "But if he does me wrong, I'll be sure to remember your offer."

They spent the rest of the day organizing perennial displays and swapping conspiracy theories on a television crime show they both followed. As was usual when she was with Chase, they laughed a lot and the time passed quickly. Del also stopped by her father's place a few times to check on Rex, who had been relegated to the house and its adjacent fenced portion of the yard outside his doggie door while her father was at work. Thankfully, each time she found him waiting at the door, eyes alert and tail wagging. But when she refused to let him out the front door, old Rex lay his head down on a soft whine.

"Sorry, Rexie, I know you hate being stuck inside all day," she told him on her late afternoon visit. "Will seeing Louie tonight help cheer you up?"

His tail thumped against the floor in double-time, so she took that as a yes.

"Perfect." Del gave him a gentle scratch behind the ears. "See you in a little bit with your buddy."

True to her word, she returned to the farm at six thirty with Isaac and Louie in tow. The bulldog wiggled with excitement the moment he saw Rex. Once they'd stepped through the fence and unclipped his lead, the excitement turned into pure glee. He bounced in circles, then sped off doing zoomies around the yard, Rex barking playfully in hot pursuit.

"What a great idea," Isaac said, pulling her into his chest. "We used to go to a dog park a few times a week out east. I know he's missed it."

They stood there in comfortable silence, watching the dogs run and play. She may have downplayed her feelings to Chase earlier, but standing here in Isaac's arms, she knew things between them had begun to run deeper than "just having fun." His touch was too familiar, her cravings for it too deep.

"Whereabout, out east?" she asked.

"New York." He released her to take the Sweet Mash carryout bag from her hands and carried it to a patio set nearby.

Okay, that was more than he'd given her before. Maybe tonight he would finally open up about his past. "The state or the city?"

"Both. I have, er, had an apartment in Lower Manhattan. Used to take the subway to work every day."

Del felt her brows rise. "Wow. Moving to Bourbon Falls must have been a serious culture shock."

He smirked. "Just a bit. Although the longer I'm here, the less I miss all the hustle and bustle. Honestly, the quiet drove me crazy the first few weeks. If it hadn't been for Louie and his frequent snoring, I may have lost my mind."

Del laughed. She joined him to help unpack their meals, thankful their paths had been destined to cross. Why else would he have turned up here, now?

"He isn't the quietest sleeper, that's for sure."

Isaac leaned closer, his lips kissing their way along the shell of her ear. "I can relegate him to the hallway if you want to stay over tonight. But I can't promise I'd let you get a full night's sleep."

A pleasant shiver washed over her. "Sleep is overrated."

"Is it, now?"

He pulled her closer, kissing his way down her neck to the top of her shoulder. Her fingers curled into his hair as more shivers followed, full of delicious anticipation. Rex and Louie barked together nearby, drawing both of their attention. Seeing nothing, she pecked a kiss on Isaac's cheek and took a step back. It'd be just her luck to have the fire squad show up so her father could check on Rex for himself. And while she'd love to introduce Isaac to Pops, having him arrive to find them making out in his backyard wouldn't make the best first impression.

"If we keep this up, our dinner's going to get cold."

"Isn't that what microwaves are for?" he asked with a shrug.

"Hey, if I'm staying over tonight, we're both gonna need food to sustain us."

At her wink, he hurried to help divvy up their orders. Soon they were seated and digging into Gina's Wednesday special: country fried steak. After the groans of pleasure from Isaac had subsided—apparently, he'd never had it before—curiosity sent her wading back into the conversation they'd started earlier.

"So did you grow up in New York City?"

Isaac took another bite of food, his gaze shifting to the dogs. "Actually, I grew up outside of Wilmington, Delaware, which is about half an hour south of Philly. I've got a sister who's eight years older than me, but we've never been all that close. The minute she left for college, my mother decided it was time for her to exit stage left as well. So my teen years were spent bouncing back and forth between two parents who were more focused on 'moving on' than raising their remaining child."

"That sounds miserable."

"Trust me, at times it was." A humorless laugh escaped him. "But it wasn't all bad. I mean, with everyone so self-absorbed, it's how I discovered my love of computers and technology. In high school, one of the tech ed teachers discovered my passion for coding, and took me under his wing. Mr. Gunnar was awesome. No matter how good or bad a day that man had, he always made sure to ask how I was doing and offer me words of encouragement. He wrote the most awesome college recommendation letters, and helped me get into Rutgers with enough scholarships that once I left home, I didn't have to go back."

"Wow," Del said. "He sounds like an amazing teacher."

"He was. I'll be forever indebted to Mr. Gunnar."

"And you don't…miss your family?" she asked, struggling to picture a world that didn't include her father, aunt, sister, and niece. Or even Hannah, though she wasn't physically here.

"Sadly, no." Isaac offered her a half smile. "My family is night and day to yours, Delaney. But in college, I made new friends and ended up rooming with the man who would eventually become my business partner, Will McManus. Our dream was to create a company that could develop affordable yet expandable apps and websites that could help small and fledgling sales companies get their businesses off the ground. We worked our asses off in college to scrape together all the money we could, and recruited a few programmers we knew that showed promise. Then, when the time was right and the market showed a solid need for the apps we'd developed, Will and I struck out and started our own IT design and services company."

Del leaned in, eager to hear more. "Did it work?"

"Let's just say we ate a lot of ramen the first year or two. But over time, our name started getting out and our reputation strengthened. A few years more, and we had people requesting our help instead of us having to go begging for work. As our workload grew, we had to hire a few more people to assist with programming and office staff. They've become my family, and I wouldn't trade them for the world."

"Then…why are you here and not there? Are you guys looking to expand?"

No sooner did she get her hopes up than he shook his head and looked away, a tension she'd not seen since those first few days around him returning.

"I wish it were that simple."

Something had gone wrong; Del could sense it. Had he and Will had a falling out? Maybe over a messy office romance? Rex perked up, which made Louie lift his head off the ground as well. It seemed everyone was on pins and needles to hear the rest of the story.

She reached for his hand. "It's okay, you can tell me."

Isaac met her gaze, searching, then looked to the yard on a sigh. "I promised I wouldn't, but…"

Del placed a hand on his cheek, turning his face back to hers. "Tell me."

"Yes, do tell," came a familiar voice behind them. Del dropped her hand in surprise as Mia stepped out from the farmhouse's backdoor. "You've been holding out on us long enough, *Robert*."

Chapter Thirteen

AND THERE IT was—the other shoe he'd been waiting to drop. Isaac fought the urge to throw up as Del retracted her hand, brows low in confusion.

"Robert?" She looked from him to Mia. "What are you talking about? And why are you even here?"

"Aunt Faye asked me to bring you her account information for the website. When your truck wasn't at home or his place, I figured I'd stop and see if it was here. Now I'm glad I did."

Mia crossed to Delaney and handed her a piece of paper, then moved to stand behind her, arms crossed and one brow arched. Isaac received the message loud and clear: big sis was here to protect her younger one. Of all the scenarios he'd run through the past few days of how to explain his past to Delaney, this hadn't been one of them.

"You could have texted," Del said to her sister in a growl.

"I might have," Mia said, "if I hadn't already been planning to have a few words with your new BF, here. By the sounds of it, though, I won't have to twist his arm after all."

Yep, just as he'd suspected. Mia may not have recognized

him the instant they'd met, but she'd gone home and done her research. Though this certainly wasn't ideal, he was relieved she hadn't spilled the beans to Del before he'd had a chance to clear the air. Hopefully, hearing it from him, she would be more inclined to believe his side of the story.

"Please, Robert," Mia encouraged. "Continue."

"Why do you keep calling him Robert?"

Del looked to Isaac, wariness now joining the confusion etched into her features. Mia, however, said nothing, her gaze remaining fixed on him. What must it be like, having an older sister willing to come to your rescue? Though, as Mia was about to find out, there was really nothing to rescue Delaney from. He just prayed they would believe him once he'd told his side of the story.

"Because that's the name most people know me by."

Del leaned away from him, and he fought the urge to resent Mia for what she'd done. It was his fault that he'd kept secrets from Del, not hers. Now it was time to make things right.

"Yes, I've kept a few things from you, Delaney. But please, before you condemn me for that, just hear me out. I've had my reasons, and this affects more people than just me. My telling you anything is breaking a promise I made to Will."

Louie, being the best friend that he was, came to rest a slobber-covered chin on his knee. Isaac pet his bully, summoning the strength he needed to go on.

"Everything I've told you tonight has been true. In fact, I haven't lied to you about anything. I just held a few things back, trying to protect the family I just told you about."

"You mean at your company," Del said, skepticism in each word.

"Yes. They got sucked into this mess because of something I did, which is why I'm here and they aren't." He drew in a deep breath and let it out slowly. "Like I said before Mia arrived, after college Will and I built our company from the ground up. We scraped together money, recruited young, talented programmers, and submitted responses to every IT-related app design bid sent out by small companies that we could find. Will went by William when scouting for work, and he convinced me to use my middle name of Robert as my business name because he thought it sounded older and more professional.

"Eventually, Manning & McManus IT Services won a few accounts. We threw everything we had into those early jobs and developed a great rapport with those clients. They told others about us, and soon we were being requested to submit proposals instead of the other way around. With more work coming in, Will's role shifted to being the face of the company, mine to verifying the plausibility of work we were quoting and to lead the programming team. Eventually, we hired some administrative staff to help keep us techies and our deadlines straight. Five years in, we dug out of the red and into the black. Proposals were being accepted, work was stacking up, and we were able to afford office space in a nicer part of the city. Everything was going great. And then Katrina came along."

"The hurricane?" Del asked.

"No, though Katrina Gibbons caused a completely different kind of storm for us—a social media storm." He shook his head. Damn this dark cloud that had found its way above him once more. "She was a courier for a company we used often when exchanging bid proposals to potential clients. You would think in this day and age that everyone would want them sent digitally, but many still require proposals be submitted in print. We were on Katrina's usual route, and she stopped by our office fairly often. We got along well, usually joking about the weather or talking sports. Then one day, she asked me out for coffee."

He could still picture that moment, her standing there in the sunshine outside their office, smiling as she teased him about his Yankees. He'd been surprised by the offer, flattered even. With her raven-black hair and smoky gray eyes, he'd always found her attractive. Finally, someone had offered him attention instead of Will.

"Go on," Del said, crossing her arms.

"I figured coffee seemed harmless enough, so we went. And we actually had a good time. So we met again for lunch the next week. And then drinks the week after. By our fourth or fifth date, though, my friends started noticing some red flags. Like her glaring at my female coworkers when my back was turned, and the way she started making plans for the both of us throughout the week. If I had to work late, she'd be there, too, bringing me dinner and staying until I was done. I just thought she was being sweet; my friends saw it as neurotic and controlling. Eventually, though, I did start to feel smothered. When she stopped by after work to see me that next week, I knew I'd be there several more hours trying to wrap up a huge proposal. I told her I'd have to catch up with her the next day. She took it better than I'd expected and wished me luck in getting done at a decent hour, then proceeded to sit outside my apartment building waiting for me to get home. I only know this because another of my friends has a place in the same building and saw her out there.

"Needless to say, when I found out she was more or less stalking me, I knew it was time to part ways. We grabbed coffee the next afternoon, and when she started laying out 'our' plans for the week, I gently suggested that maybe it was time we saw other people. She demanded to know who had caught my eye, and I was honest in saying there wasn't anyone, but work was getting busier and I really didn't see this thing between us going anywhere. Katrina looked down at her empty coffee cup, crushed it in one hand, then threw it in my face and told me I'd regret making a fool of her in front of the other patrons."

"After she threw her coffee cup at you," Del said, eyes narrowed. "Lovely woman."

"It gets worse," her sister murmured.

Yep, Mia had done her homework.

"Much worse," he agreed. "A few days later, Will comes rushing into the office, freaking out about a Twitter post that'd gone viral overnight containing a video of me from a Giants game Katrina and I had gone to the weekend prior. In it, I was shown going off about how women were idiots and should never have left *the* kitchen. The post questioned our company values and hashtagged us as misogynists and corporate pigs."

"Did you really say those things?" Mia asked.

Isaac hesitated, knowing things were about to get tricky.

"Yes," he said, watching their eyes widen as expected. "And no. See, I'd worn my favorite Eli Manning jersey to the game that day. And while I was making my way to the concession stand after the first quarter, a group of six or seven highly intoxicated women came stumbling through the order area. They all had on matching T-shirts advertising someplace over in Hell's Kitchen, and one had a sash advertising her as a 'Bride to Be.' Anyway, they were being absolute jerks, shoving their way through the crowd. One of them lost their footing and toppled into a waiting customer, causing a domino effect in the already congested space. Trays went flying. I managed to catch the wife of an older couple just before she face-planted onto the concrete floor, but her husband wasn't so lucky. He went down hard on his left knee, and their tray full of drinks and cheese-covered nachos rained all over me.

"Needless to say, I was livid, not just because of my jersey, but because the drunks were being horrendous and people were getting hurt. I flagged down security, who caught up with the intoxicated group and tossed them out before anyone else got hurt. By the time I finally made it back to our seats, I'd missed most of the second quarter. I didn't know it at the time, but Katrina recorded me going off to the guys sitting around us about how those women should have never been let into the game and how they never should never have left *Hell's* Kitchen."

Del frowned. "I don't get it. Why would you, going off about idiot drunks, be such a bad thing?"

"It probably wouldn't have been if she'd left the video alone. But she tampered with it, editing out half the words to make it sound like I was bashing all women and suggesting they should never have left the kitchen. Here, I'll show you."

Despite Katrina's insistence that she knew little about computers, she'd been savvy enough with whatever video editing app she had on her cell phone to create a plausible new clip. To a casual observer, the splices were hardly noticeable. After pairing the short video with a handful of trending sexual discrimination hashtags, she easily pulled the wool over the Twitterverse's eyes. Isaac pulled her tweet up on his phone and played it for them, watching their faces closely for a reaction. Would they believe his story or Katrina's?

"Man, you were mad." Del's gaze roved from the screen to him and back. She hit play again, then Mia did the same. "But why would a single tweet send you running from the Big Apple?"

Isaac grimaced. "It might not have if Will and I had kept our mouths shut. But the tweet got shared thousands of times, and soon people weren't just hating on me but also on our company. We tried to defend ourselves, pointing out the slight lag in the video at the two- and ten-second marks, but we'd already been deemed guilty by the court of Twitter. Things got really ugly, really fast."

"So, what happened next?" Del asked. "Did you confront her? Because you know damn well, I would have."

"Yes, but—Wait, does this mean you believe me?"

Del exchanged a confused look with her sister. "Well, yeah. In all the time I've known you, you've never once said anything derogatory about women. And you're right—if you watch the clip enough, you can see those tiny lags in the video. So, why wouldn't we believe you?"

He slumped back into his seat as the weight of the world lifted off his shoulders. "Because several hundred thousand other people didn't."

"Wow. Then clearly there's a lot of idiots in the world. Now get back to the story. What happened next?"

He smirked. Her tenacity was awesome. What had he done to deserve a girlfriend like her?

"Well, like I said, Will absolutely freaked out. When

Katrina refused to take the video down, we called the staff in and showed it to them. Wanted to get everything on the table so they could ask me any questions they might have. I can't tell you what a relief it was to hear them denounce her and pledge to stand by me while we figured this mess out. After a long discussion, we decided that the best next move was not to provoke her further and see if the fire would put itself out. That was before *The View* picked up on it and aired a short feature about corporate bullying. And of course, they tossed one of our new hashtags into the commentary."

Del and Mia grimaced.

"Yeah, it wasn't pretty. The following Monday, we lost our first client. By midweek, three more were threatening to cancel their contracts and five future clients revoked our bid submittals. Fearing our company was on the verge of collapse, I volunteered to disappear for a while. Will's aunt and uncle had left him this place years ago, so it seemed the logical choice. I've been able to work remotely while the rest of the team carries on. Will hired a PR firm to help craft simple statements denying the allegations, and the general public thinks Robert Manning is still on sabbatical."

"So what you're saying is, you're only hiding out in Bourbon Falls until all of this blows over," Mia said.

Leave it to Mia to cut to the chase.

He looked to Del, who now sat still as stone. As much as he hated to admit the truth, there was no point in lying while trying to earn her trust. "Yes."

DEL ROSE FROM her seat and began to pace along her father's back patio, waiting for the shock of Isaac's confession to subside. His moving here was just…temporary? When exactly had he planned to tell her this?

She looked to Mia, who was watching her closely. Probably because she expected Del to flip out like she had when she'd found out about Jonathan and his other life. And while, yes, Isaac had kept secrets from her, this was different. Jonathan had knowingly been living dual lives—who knows, maybe even more than that—stringing multiple women along. His actions had been driven by greed and arrogance. Isaac was living two lives, haunted by fear and the stupid social media. So, unless some secret fiancée popped up out of the bushes, Del had no reason to flip out. In truth, she felt badly for Isaac…and a whole lot of rage toward this crazy Katrina woman.

"Of course, if Will finds out I've told you this, he'll go ballistic."

"Then why risk it?" Del asked.

"Because not telling you was starting to eat me alive. Will and I agreed not to tell anyone outside our company about this, not just to protect me but the whole team. That's why I've been hiding at my place all these months—I was trying *not* to meet anyone so there'd be no chance of me breaking that promise. But then Brooklyn came sliding into my landscaping, and her protective aunt came charging in to save her."

"For which I am entirely grateful." Mia sighed. "I'm sorry that you've been publicly and unfairly dragged through the mud, Isaac. Thank you for sharing your story with us. And please forgive me for barging in on your dinner. After putting two and two together at the bookstore the other night, my protective big sister mode kicked into overdrive. I've seen Del get hurt by lies before, and I worried it was happening all over again. If there's anything I can do to help, please count me in."

"Thanks, Sis."

"Thank you, Mia. And I don't blame you for wanting to protect Del. I've been trying to do that, too."

Once Mia had gone, Isaac rose and came to stand before Del, blocking her path. She stared at his chest, too chicken to look him in the eyes. Because those warm, brown eyes of his would be silently asking for her forgiveness and understanding. And she, caring deeply for him like she did, would offer him both, even if his story's underlying message was a hard pill to swallow.

Isaac wasn't staying.

"You've been hurt by lies before?"

Del grimaced. As if her mind wasn't churning enough already, now Mia had dropped that little tidbit before leaving. But she didn't want to dredge out old, unpleasant memories; she wanted to be in the here and now, before the relationship rug got yanked out from under once again. She stepped around him to take a seat on the patio's top step. Isaac followed, settling onto the space beside her.

"Let's just say the guy I was seeing after college wasn't entirely forthcoming with his plans for the future."

"You mean like holding out on not wanting to get married or have kids?"

She snorted. If only it'd been something that simple.

"Oh, he had every intention of getting married, just not to me. It takes a special kind of assholery to lead double lives, wooing two women at the same time. He claimed he did a lot of traveling for work, which was true. What he didn't tell me about was the woman living in the other city to where he often traveled who came from high society and would nicely complete his stock portfolio. Just as I started thinking he was the one, Mia brought me an engagement announcement she'd found online. Jonathan's name was listed...with someone other than me."

Isaac's hands fisted. "Seriously? How can a person do that and be able to sleep at night?"

"Dunno, but he did without losing a wink. Needless to say, I wasn't the most trusting person for a long time. You know, fool me once, shame on you; fool me twice, shame on me."

"Nothing about that was your fault," Isaac said.

"Oh, there were red flags with him, just like there were for you with Katrina. I just chose to ignore them, thought I was being paranoid."

"I can appreciate that." Isaac looked out over the backyard on a sigh. "I'm sorry I wasn't honest with you from the start, Delaney. I was scared for my company, scared for my friends. If M&M goes under because of my failed relationship, I'll never forgive myself."

"I know," she grumbled, leaning into his side. Even now, she avoided his eyes, not yet ready to set aside her anger at the unfairness of it all. "But this whole thing is stupid. And you guys wonder why I hate the internet."

"It's not all bad," he said. "The website we built together might be what saves your family's bookstore."

See? Fate. Without Isaac here, the website never would have happened.

So why would fate bring him to her, only to turn around and yank him away?

"How long?" she asked quietly.

"I don't know. Could be months, could be days." He pulled her closer, his chin coming to rest atop her crown. "Funny, a month ago I couldn't wait for this all to be over. Now, all I want is for time to come to a stop."

"Why?"

"Because of you." He shifted to lift her chin, his gaze searching hers. "I thought I was done with dating, done with baring my soul to others. Then you came along in your big ole pickup and marched through my yard like you own the place."

"And yet you're not planning on staying."

His smile saddened. "They need me back home."

But I need you here. Whoa, where did that come from? She most definitely didn't *need* anyone.

Del rose and started cleaning up their dinner plates. She'd been through breakups before; it'd be foolish to think she'd never go through another. Though, this wasn't exactly a breakup, now was it? More like a ticking clock.

And she'd be damned if she was going to waste their finite time together moping and being angry at the world. She'd watched her father do that all these years, and his anger had gotten him nowhere. She refused to do the same.

"Then I guess we'd better get this website up and running before Will calls and steals you back."

"Oh, I promise not to leave before we get that rolling," Isaac said. "No way am I going to let that masterpiece go to waste."

"Good, because I promised Aunt Faye I would find a way to save the bookstore. Getting to work on it with you was just an unexpected bonus."

She flashed him a forced smile, before the image of him leaving had a chance to surface in her mind. That was something she wasn't ready to process, and honestly didn't know if she ever would be. Isaac had touched her heart in ways no one else ever had. And while she knew they weren't headed for the altar, Del sensed this was one relationship she might never completely heal from.

"We haven't eaten our cobbler yet." She looked to Isaac. "Still hungry?"

"I mean, it *is* Gina's famous cobbler," he answered with a sheepish grin. "I'd sure hate to see it go to waste."

Del mock-gasped. "Go to waste? Why, that'd be sacrilege."

His resulting smile had her smiling in return. *See?* This was the kind of thing she would miss about him—his contagious smiles and shared love of dessert. Even so, she should have known better than to think this would last. They were just having fun, which was far better than the boredom she'd been experiencing for quite a while. She just hoped she could keep her brain and her heart separate on this one.

Del dished out two servings of cobbler and took her seat beside him, then shifted her gaze to the dogs; they'd both been snoozing since Isaac finished telling his woeful tale. Heck, even Louie was becoming part of their family. She hated to see either of them head back to the East Coast, before they'd had time to really give this relationship a chance.

Maybe he didn't need to go back.

Hadn't Isaac said he'd been working remotely all these months? From what it sounded like, their company was still afloat. So maybe he just *thought* his team needed him back in NYC because that was their original plan and he'd not thought about it any further.

Perhaps she could find a way to convince him that working out here was actually a trial run. That wouldn't be enough, though. He had to want to stay. Really want it, if he was going to give up the Big Apple.

So how could she make that happen?

Her mind replayed their earlier conversation, before Mia had arrived. Hadn't he said something about his family and how different their dynamic was from hers? That he hadn't had the same loving, supportive environment she had growing up? If his coworkers had become his family, then it was no wonder he longed to go back. But what if Del helped him see what more there was to be had in life, what it felt like to be part of a loving family and a close-knit community? Maybe then he would change his mind about going back and be open to the idea of continuing to work remotely while staying here, with her.

It was a longshot and a gamble, but if she didn't try changing his mind, she'd always sit back and wonder what if. And if her family had taught her anything over the years, it was that life was too damn short for what ifs. Del had spent years doing all she could to help everyone else. Now it was time to fight for what *she* wanted.

And what she wanted most right now was to save the bookstore...and for Isaac to stay.

One thing at a time. She bumped her elbow to his. "So are we gonna get this bad boy rolling tonight or what?"

"The website?" Isaac asked. "We can certainly give it a

try. It just depends on whether or not Mia brought us everything we need. We'll have to go back to my place, though. I didn't bring my laptop with me."

"Your place?" she echoed. "Hmm, that might work out nicely. Quite nicely indeed."

"Why's that?"

Offering him a demure look, she reached over and trailed her fingers delicately up his forearm. "It's the perfect place to celebrate our success once the website goes live."

Isaac met her gaze, his darkening with desire. In two forkfuls, he finished his cobbler and jumped to his feet. "Well, we better get over there. Time's a wasting, after all."

Del couldn't agree more.

Chapter Fourteen

DEL AWOKE TO her cell phone vibrating on the nightstand. She cracked one eyelid open, realized there was a snoring dog blocking her path, and blew out a sigh. God bless Louie, he wasn't giving up his place in Isaac's bed. She slithered past his brawny body as best she could and grabbed her phone, surprised at the time—three a.m. again; her alarm wasn't due to go off for another three hours—but not nearly as surprised as the incoming message from Margaret.

Our first application came in!

Del smiled at the screen before her. She'd had her doubts these past few weeks, unsure that their talent show idea would ever get off the ground. But Isaac had done an amazing job with their website, and had been entirely optimistic when they launched it last night. He'd gone on and on about SE-something, which he was supposedly a wizard at; Del honestly had cared less in that moment about the magic he'd made on his keyboard and more about the magic they were about to make together in his bed. Now pride swelled in her chest at her man's skills and what they could mean to the bookstore.

She propped herself up on one elbow and texted back.

Fantastic!

Yes, all we need is another twenty-nine more. Now get your fanny home—it's late and we have work to do.

Del softly groaned. Margaret frequently forgot that not everyone kept the hours she did.

Sleep first, then work, then our meeting tonight. Bring your ideas and excitement with you.

Spoiled sport.

On a grunt, Del laid back down. Unfortunately, with the realization that this talent show was really going to happen, her mind refused to quiet. She stretched to kiss Isaac on the cheek and whispered, "I'm heading out. Thanks again for last night."

His arm circled her waist, keeping her from slipping away. "It's still dark. Stay."

"Can't sleep, I should go."

His eyes found hers in the dark. "Something wrong?"

"Nope, the opposite." She held up her phone. "Margaret texted—we got our first applicant!"

A sleepy smile stretched across his lip. "I told you SEO was the key."

"Well, I'm glad one of us is a freaking web design genius."

Isaac shifted to curl his other arm around her and nuzzled the soft spot beneath her ear. "You know what this calls for?"

Del shivered at his touch, her body coming alive at the possibilities. "No, what?"

"More celebration sex."

"Excellent suggestion." She shifted closer, her lips seeking his. "Count me in."

HALF AN HOUR later and now *far* too awake to sleep, she pulled into her driveway and made for the back door.

"I knew you wouldn't be able to go back to sleep."

Del spun to find Margaret leaning over her fence, a coffee cup in hand and smug grin on her lips. Though it was muggy and warm even at this early hour, the older woman had on a thin, fleece house coat over a two-piece pajama set. Del had no doubt she was also wearing her purple fuzzy slippers. Mrs. Harper was predictable, if nothing else.

"Hard to do when you're getting texts at all hours of the night."

"Bah, you'll get plenty of sleep when you start your dirt nap. Only got a few weeks to get this event off the ground."

She had a point. Del felt her anxiety begin to grow. But just how much could they do at this hour?

Too awake—and now also too worried—to go back to sleep, she invited Margaret in and started a fresh pot of coffee. Neither mentioned Del's very late arrival home, though the older woman's continued smirk said enough. As

Margaret pulled a small notepad and pen from her house coat, Del remembered she was sitting with a former reporter. She topped off the other woman's coffee cup, filled one for herself, then joined Mrs. Harper at her kitchen banquette.

"Can I ask you something news related?"

"Absolutely. What's on your mind, kid?"

"Well, hypothetically, if something were to come out in the news that…tainted someone's reputation, but it wasn't true even though lots of people believed it was, how do you go about fixing all that?"

Margaret smiled at her over the rim of her coffee cup. "You're talking about Robert Manning and that ridiculous video his ex-girlfriend posted."

Del's jaw dropped. "You *knew*?!"

"Of course I knew. Do you really think I don't research people new to our area? Who else is going to make sure we don't have serial killers or child molesters land in Bourbon Falls?"

"Oh my goodness, Margaret." If she was so good at researching everyone, why hadn't she given Del the heads up on Jonathan? Then again, she hadn't given her the heads up on Isaac, either. Most likely, she knew about both…which meant Margaret was much better at keeping secrets than Del realized. "So what did you think of the video?"

"Pfft, total hack job. I could have done better myself if I knew how." She took a long sip of her coffee. "Unfortunately, there're a lot of idiots in this world, sitting around waiting for a bandwagon to jump on. Throw out the right buzzwords, and they're quick to climb on board."

Del shook her head. This was precisely why she avoided the internet and social media. Sure, there were great causes and real news out there, but how would she ever know what was truth and what wasn't? Poor Isaac, thinking he was on a harmless date and suddenly finding himself in a mess gone viral.

"So how do you go about fixing that kind of slander?"

"Well, some people play ostrich like your honey bunny did, duck their head in the sand and wait for the storm to pass. Others ignore it and go about their lives. Oftentimes those are the ones hoping for any kind of attention: good, bad, or a mix of both. The third group tries to fight it, though that can obviously go bad in a hurry if they can't win the sympathy of the audience following along with the drama."

Apparently, Margaret didn't know about their failed attempt at first, choosing door number three. And since door number two hadn't worked, they'd eventually been forced through door number one.

"Isaac and his business partner have been trying to protect their company; they don't want it to fold and leave the rest of their coworkers out on the street."

"That's why he moved out here?" At Del's nod, Margaret added, "So he takes one for the team, moves out here, and then meets the woman of his dreams but is stuck playing hermit."

"Not sure I'm the woman of his dreams, but yeah, something like that."

Margaret arched a brow. "The man built you a website to help save your family bookstore."

"He built *us* a website to save the bookstore."

"But he told you about the mess he's hiding from, no?"

Del shrugged. "Last night, when Mia called him out on it."

"So he just put his entire company's future on the line rather than keep you in the dark?" Margaret snorted softly. "Enough said."

It did have a nice ring to it. "But he says he's not staying."

"I'll believe that when I see it," Margaret said.

"How can you be so sure?"

"When you live as long as I have and have seen the things I've seen, you develop one hell of an intuition. It's rarely wrong. Even so…"

Del watched her neighbor, the gears clearly turning. "What are you thinking?"

"I'm thinking we've only got one option: party at my place so I can watch and assess. Then you'll have an answer."

"Oh, geez. Not sure I'm ready for that." Or that Isaac was ready for that.

"If my intuition is correct, you'll be happy with the outcome." Margaret rose with a wink. "Saturday night, six o'clock potluck. We'll win him over with our small-town charm."

"But what if he won't come?"

"His loss. Just make sure to bring my favorite snacks; we'll have a good time without him."

Del laughed. "You're incorrigible."

"Nope, just love my snacks."

She thanked Margaret for the chat, then watched to make sure she made it safely back to her side of the fence before shifting her thoughts to the upcoming weekend. A neighborhood party—it fell perfectly in line with her plan to help Isaac learn what it felt like to be part of a supportive community of family and friends. But would he agree to come?

Then again, if he learned his secret was already out, then there really wasn't any reason not to.

"A PARTY?"

Isaac lowered his fork, the leftover dessert Del had brought to tonight's planning meeting sliding off its tines. He'd spent a good part of Thursday second-guessing his decision to tell Del and Mia his story, but sometime around dinner had come to the conclusion he'd done the right thing. Now he was starting to second-guess anew.

"Del, what part of 'we need to keep my being here secret'

did you not follow last night?"

"I know, I know, but it honestly wasn't my idea. It was Margaret Harper's, which she tossed out after admitting she'd, um, already figured out your identity."

"She *what*?!"

"I know, right? Totally crazy. But she's also a former reporter and wicked smart—which is one of the reasons we keep her included in everything. You know, since she'll figure it all out eventually anyway."

Isaac pushed his plate away, appetite gone. Will had warned him that word would get out if he started mingling with the locals. But had he listened to the man? Oh no. Now he was going to have to call him up and eat some serious crow. And move again. Or maybe just live out of his car. No, that wouldn't work; he needed an internet connection and someplace to work.

"You're panicking."

He met Del's knowing gaze. "Hell yes, I'm panicking. I've been sitting in this house for seven months now, trying not to be found. Now half the town seems to know I'm here."

"Four people is hardly half the town."

"Four?" he cried. "I thought it was only three!"

"You're forgetting Brooklyn."

Four people going on forty. He looked to the living room, wondering how long it would take him to pack his essentials and hit the road. But where would he even go? To his mom's or dad's? Or maybe his sister's place? He cringed, imagining how that conversation might go.

"Isaac." Del came to stand before him. "I know you aren't used to having family who supports you, but that's what we do in Bourbon Falls—we love and support one another. And whether you like it or not, you're one of us. This party Saturday? It's to celebrate the launch of our website. The website *you* built. No one there believes Katrina's crazy story, and no one will go telling the world you're here. They just want to save our bookstore and have a little fun along the way."

Isaac shook his head. Going was a bad idea. Why hadn't he just stuck to the plan? "I…can't."

"Can't?" she asked softly. "Or won't?"

He met her pleading gaze, torn. Del had been so giving to him, so selfless since the day they met. Clearly, this party was important to her. But what if the others didn't keep their word?

A knot formed in his stomach. He was no longer in control of keeping his whereabouts secret. Then again, if her neighbor truly had already figured it out, she might not be the only one. Which meant, in truth, he likely never did.

"I shouldn't," he whispered, his resolve wavering.

Del's hands cupped his cheeks. "No, honey. You absolutely should. And I promise you, your secret is safe with us. Our Bourbon Falls family takes care of our own, and you're a part of that now."

She was right—he hadn't come from a supportive, loving family. He came from one where individual priorities and ambitions outweighed those of the collective. It was difficult to imagine there being another way, yet here was Del, promising exactly that. Isaac pulled her into his chest, seeking strength from the woman who always seemed to have plenty.

"You can even bring Louie," she said, wrapping her arms around him. "I'd love to have you both stay over. And have I mentioned I make a mean French toast?"

Now she wasn't playing fair.

"French toast?" He kissed her neck. "How can I say no to that?"

Del stayed over that night, her presence and her touch helping to soothe his anxiety. Though he'd always been a bit of an introvert, staying away from society these past months had made him even more so. Thankfully, his date for Saturday was as extroverted as they came. Surely, she would help balance him out.

With his elevated workload, and a growing number of daily texts from his staff, Friday went by in a blink and suddenly Saturday evening was staring him in the face. Before he knew it, he was pulling his SUV into a paved driveway amid a row of well-kept Craftsman homes and other assorted bungalows. Yards were small but neat and tidy, and shared a common sidewalk that ran the length of the block. Her entire street had a cozy feel to it, and Isaac found himself green with envy.

His minimalistic apartment in New York City was nothing like this.

Del's home was painted a subtle green—sage, would be his guess—with cream-colored columns and matching wooden shutters. Her front porch looked as inviting as its owner always was, adorned with numerous hanging and potted plants. A chain-strung swing hung to the left of her front door, its style and color matching the shutters. Though similar homes lined the street, Isaac felt drawn to hers the most. As he exited his vehicle to take it all in, Del stepped out from a side door and came to greet him.

"You found it." She stretched to give him a soft welcome kiss. "Welcome to Casa de Del."

"Your home is gorgeous. And about a million times nicer looking than my rental. You must feel like you've been slumming it with me these past few weeks."

"Not in the least. And you're only seeing it as it is now. When I bought it, this place was in sad disrepair. It took many months and many helping hands to get it restored, inside and out. But it was totally worth it—I couldn't be happier with how it turned out. I'll give you the grand tour later."

He nodded, his gaze shifting to the fenced-in backyard. Was that a pergola with string lights back there? "Can't wait to see it."

"You ready?" she asked, tipping her head toward the collection of voices coming from the backyard next door. A four-foot wooden fence separated Del's yard from theirs, an entry gate to the other yard standing a few paces away. Once he passed through that gate, there'd be no turning back.

He grimaced. "I'd like to say I was."

"You'll do great." She took his hand and gave it a reassuring squeeze. "And good news, you won't be the only guy here. Robyn's husband, Drew, came. He's super chill and loves to talk baseball. So does Chase, who said he'd try to make it after a bit. And Nan Harrington's husband, Harold, is in there—if you're a card player, you two will totally hit it off."

Cards and baseball, both doable topics. Even so, knowing more people would be here instead of fewer didn't exactly lower his anxiety.

"And you're sure they're not going to go and, you know..."

"Tattle on you?" Del laughed. "No, I'm pretty sure Drew and Harold would rather poke themselves in the eye than get involved in media drama. Now grab Louie and let's get in there. We'll hang out with everyone for a while, then head back to my place for the rest of the night."

She waggled her brows, the implication sending Isaac into motion. It'd been a few weeks since their first time together, but the fires hadn't cooled. If anything, they'd heated up.

Damn, he was going to miss that.

Oh, who was he kidding? He was going to miss all of her, from those bright-blue eyes and welcoming smile, to the way she always gave so freely of herself to meet everyone's needs. Tonight, he hoped to help meet her needs, too, by being at her side and joining in on the celebration.

Isaac helped Louie from his vehicle, then looped arms with Del and let her lead the way.

"Here goes nothing," he said. *And everything.*

Chapter Fifteen

DEL SAT WITH Mia, Brooklyn, Robyn, Barbara, and Margaret, watching Isaac interact with the others from across the yard. She knew he'd been nervous about tonight, and for the first few minutes he'd kept a firm grip on her offered hand. But once Drew started razzing him about his Yankees cap, he'd relaxed and ventured off to engage in baseball banter. Now he sat at a card table with Drew, Chase, Harold, and Nan, dealing out a hand of Texas Hold'em with an easy smile on his face. As she watched, he caught her gaze from across the way and gave her a wink.

"Looks like your man is enjoying himself," Margaret said over the top of her red Solo cup.

"Yes, it does." She clinked her cup to Margaret's. "The party was a great idea."

"Parties are always great ideas," said Mia, who had broken out a bottle of her favorite wine and appeared to be feeling no pain. With Mia, it didn't take much. She issued a happy, wine-infused sigh. "I'm so glad Aunt Faye finally made it. I was starting to worry."

"You, worry?" Del teased. She received a dark look from

her tipsy sister. "Yes, I'm glad she made it, too. Stinks that Pops had to work and couldn't join us, though."

"I agree," Robyn said. "Your dad always cracks me up when he gets to drinking."

"Which is why we try to keep that to a minimum," Mia said. "That man can't hold his liquor."

Which, apparently, he'd passed down to her. The rest of their group exchanged a look with Del, who just shook her head and smiled.

"So what all do we have left to do ahead of the talent show? We've got food vendors lined up, and those two awesome food trucks from Fort Wayne agreed to make the drive—that'll be huge. And Max agreed to handle the beverage tent."

"Plus, he's giving us most of the proceeds, which was very sweet of him," added Mia who, they all knew without her ever having to say it, had always harbored a secret crush on Max Williams. But Max was happily married, which meant that crush wasn't going anywhere.

"Right, very sweet of him," Del said. "And Robyn, you and Faye were rock stars this week, getting those two, huge new sponsors. Isaac said he'd add their logos to the website this weekend."

"It took some heartstring tugging, but Faye eventually won them over," Robyn said. "She's got another one on the fence; I'll be following up with them on Monday."

"Excellent." Margaret nodded. "Sounds to me like all we

have left to do now is a whole lotta waiting: waiting to see if we get enough applicants and sell enough tickets."

"Not if," said Aunt Faye, returning from the food table. "*When*. And we're still trying to line up a portable stage for the land next to the old depot. I've got a few feelers out, should know more later this week."

Del clinked her cup to Faye's as she took the seat beside her. "Fantastic. Great work, everyone."

As the conversation continued, Del scanned the faces around her. Aside from her father and Hannah, and the Picketts who'd already stopped by and left, all her favorite people were here and appeared to be having a wonderful time. Now all she had to do was figure out how to keep things this way.

"I just hope Isaac will still be here for the show," Mia said, reading her mind.

"Me too."

"Why wouldn't he be?" Brooklyn asked.

"Because they might call him back to work before then," Mia said, pouting. Yep, she was definitely further into that wine bottle than Del had thought. "Until then, he's gotta lay low."

"Because of the video you told me about?" Brooklyn frowned. "I thought it wasn't supposed to be all that good."

"It was good enough that a ton of people saw it and believed it, so he's been kinda stuck hiding from everyone," Del said.

"Then just make a new one that shows it was fake."

Margaret elbowed Del in the side. "Now there's a good idea. You tell 'em how it's done, kiddo."

"You really don't know?"

Brooklyn grabbed her phone and held it up, recording the card game across the lawn for several seconds. Then she tapped her phone and brought up an app Delaney hadn't heard of before. Though, in all fairness, Del hadn't heard of most of them. On purpose.

"So, you just pick your video here, and then tap where you want to add audio over the top of it. When the microphone icon comes up, you tap to start recording your voice, then again to stop recording. Watch."

Within minutes, Brooklyn had added her commentary of the card game over the top of the original video. It was downright scary, how easy she made it look.

It also reinforced Del's desire to stay off the internet and away from social media.

"See? It's so simple, pretty much anyone can do it."

"But can you overwrite any video or just ones you record?" Mia asked.

"Any," Brooklyn said with a shrug. "People snatch clips and edit with their voiceovers all the time. That's literally half the videos on TikTok right now."

"So you're saying any of us could grab the video and add a voiceover, explaining that Katrina tampered with the original one?" Robyn asked.

"Well, *I* could. I'm not sure Aunt Del could handle it." Brooklyn offered her a sheepish grin.

"And Aunt Del isn't going anywhere near this video stuff," she replied, giving Margaret a stern look. "They've gotten Isaac into enough trouble as it is. The last thing he needs is more drama. Though, I'm not gonna lie—I'd love to see Karma bite Katrina in the butt."

Brooklyn took an incoming call from her bestie and wandered off, angling for Mia's house one yard back. Del watched her go. How would her niece learn to separate the truth from the lies, growing up in a digital age where reality could be blurred so easily?

A collective groan erupted at the card table, and Del looked over to see Harold raking a pile of poker chips in his direction. The others rose from their seats, joking with one another as they shook hands and bumped fists. Louie, however, remained half passed out under the card table. He'd long since worn himself out from all the excitement of meeting new people.

"Sounds like the party's about to wrap up," Margaret said. She tipped her head to Del. "You might as well get your man and his sleepy pooch over to your house. Don't worry, I'll try not to listen too closely to any noises coming from across the fence."

Del felt her cheeks warm as the others pretended to look the other way. "You're terrible. You know that, right?"

"You wouldn't want me any other way," she replied with

a wink.

So true.

"So what's your assessment, anyway?" Del asked quietly.

"I'd put it at twenty percent."

Del felt like she'd been sucker-punched. "That he'll stay?"

"No, dummy, that he'll leave. Of course, that number could dip lower if you keep him happy in the bedroom." She shrugged. "I'm just saying."

Hope rose in Del's chest once more. The bedroom thing she could handle, but just how low she could get his probability of leaving was yet to be seen. In the back of her mind, she still had her doubts. Major doubts.

But right now, giving him reason to stay sounded a whole lot more fun.

ISAAC STAYED THE night at Del's place Saturday, then spent the better part of his Sunday there as well. She'd given him an abbreviated tour last night after the party, in too big a hurry to start their own party for two. Not that he'd complained in the least, because it was one hellova party.

A party that'd lasted All. Night. Long.

But after the sun had come up, they'd both managed to get a couple hours of sleep, and all articles of previously discarded clothing having been found, she'd taken him on the grand tour. He loved the inside of her home, such a sunny, inviting space—a stark comparison to the rental he was staying at. And her backyard was amazing, with its custom pergola, cushion-laden seating, and enclosed, fenced-in area.

Needless to say, Louie, too, had been in heaven.

Now Isaac sat snuggled next to Del on her outdoor loveseat, contemplating a nap while enjoying his own slice of heaven. He'd never wanted a home of his own, always picturing himself too busy with work to have time to deal with things like cutting the lawn or maintaining fences. But here, now, he could picture it, him lounging on a back porch like this. Maybe with a beer in one hand and a wife holding his other.

Whoa. Had he really just imagined the *W* word?

"You're awfully quiet this afternoon," Del said. "Whatcha got rattling around that noggin of yours?"

He grinned, not ready to admit that thought aloud.

"Just enjoying the change in scenery. And the company."

"She's enjoying finally having you here, too. Not that I don't like your place," she quickly added.

"Oh, you don't have to try to spare my feelings—I like your place much better than mine. In fact, I may never go back."

She laughed. "Whatever. You'd miss your recliner. And your laptop."

"True." He took a drink of the sweet tea she'd made

them earlier, trying to stay cool on another warm, early fall day. "A comfortable, reliable recliner is hard to come by."

Not as hard to come by as a woman like Delaney. If only there was a way to convince her to go back east with him. Though, she'd probably be miserable out there without a house of her own and a backyard like this. Heck, he couldn't even imagine how much it would cost to replicate what she had there or how far from the city such a property would sit. He'd spend hours commuting back and forth each day.

To keep her with him, though, it'd be worth it.

"Could you ever leave Bourbon Falls?"

"Why would I?" she asked, reaching for her glass. "My whole world is here."

He'd expected her to say as much. "But what if everything weren't right here? What if you woke up one day and realized there was more waiting for you out there?"

"I guess I hope I never wake up with that realization, because I can't imagine ever leaving my hometown. Too many people here count on me, you know?"

He did know, all too well.

"That doesn't mean you can't travel from time to time. Go on some adventures."

"I used to travel." She stared into her drink. "When I was seeing Jonathan, he took me to all sorts of places. Some historic, some exotic. I developed a pretty bad case of wanderlust there for a while. And I loved the traveling and adventures we went on, but deep down I knew I'd always come back home. I think that's probably the reason he ultimately chose her over me."

"I can't say why he did what he did, nor can I imagine being able to live with myself, leading you on like he did. But there's one thing I am absolutely certain of."

She met his gaze. "What's that?"

"He chose wrong, and I'm selfishly glad that he did."

A smile tugged at her perfect pink lips. "Me too. It took a while, but eventually I was able to see I'd dodged a major bullet when he skipped town. The man snored louder than anyone I know."

"Worse than me?"

"You don't snore. Now, Louie, on the other hand…"

Isaac's bulldog looked up from underneath the chair across from them, his preferred napping spot for the afternoon, and snorted in their direction.

"Yes, I'm talking about you, buddy." Her cell phone vibrated with an alert on the end table beside her, and she twisted to reach for it. "Hmm, what are you doing next Sunday?"

Isaac shrugged. "Depends on if you kick me out or let me crash here forever."

"Stop," she laughed. "I'm trying to be serious."

"Me too." He pulled a cushion from the adjacent seat and hugged it to his chest. "I'm having a love affair with your upholstery."

"You're a nutcase," she said. "And also, you just got invited to my father's cookout next Saturday."

A family cookout? Because what, attending a party yesterday with most of her closest friends hadn't been stressful enough? "That sounds tasty. And intimidating."

"Nah, Pops is a big pushover. Unless you work for him. Or with him. Or aren't directly related to him." She paused to consider what she'd said, then waved the thought away. "Anyway, if you're there with me, you'll be fine. But there's no pressure to say yes; I'm just extending the invite."

Like he could really tell her no. The woman had him completely wrapped around her little finger. The grin on her face only proved she knew it, too.

"Let's see how the week goes. Will's been sending me more work lately, and we've got a few big proposal deadlines coming—"

Now his cell phone was buzzing.

"Speak of the devil."

The text from Will was more frantic than usual, asking for help on a proposal that needed to go out first thing Tuesday morning. So much for enjoying a lazy Labor Day. On a sigh, he told Will to send the document in question over. It would look suspicious if his answer was anything but.

"I'm guessing that means you're heading out."

He offered Del an apologetic smile. "Unfortunately, it does."

Another text came across from Will then, this one on a

different topic. *Dude, check this out.*

A video link appeared, Katrina's face in tiny preview clip. That, he would wait to watch until later. No sense in ruining an otherwise perfect afternoon.

"Guess that means our nap is out." Del studied her cuticles. "And the post-nap aerobics."

Isaac grew hard at the implication. Damn, his girl was insatiable.

"I'm afraid duty calls." He tossed the cushion he'd been holding aside and rose before he gave her offer too much thought. Lord knew he'd much rather stay with her than go home and work.

The thought brought a smile to his face. Him, preferring to lounge than work? He never thought he'd see the day. Even more surprising was how happy that option made him feel.

"Hopefully, I can get this knocked out and things will calm down by tomorrow. Your shop is closed tomorrow, right?"

"Yes, sir. No laboring on Labor Day for us. If people want plants that badly on a holiday, they can drive to the big box stores in Warsaw. So if you get done working and want some company, let me know. Oh, and don't forget about those new sponsor logos we need added to our website. Will you still have time to do that?"

He helped her up from the loveseat and pecked a quick kiss on her cheek. Anything longer would waver his resolve.

And with Will waiting for a response, wavering was not a good option right now. "Absolutely. I'll do that as soon as I get home, before I get submerged in whatever Will sent over. Come on, Louie. Time to go for a ride."

He signed his version of *ride* to Louie, who shimmied out from under the chair he'd been using for shade and started his happy wiggle dance.

"It's too bad he doesn't enjoy car rides." Del laughed.

"I know. Guess I should take him out more often."

She smiled and gave him a knowing look. "You're welcome to stop by with him anytime."

Isaac kissed her on the nose, resisting the urge to pull her in for a more thorough kissing. Work first, then play. As much as he was enjoying playing, he did still have a company to keep afloat and employees to pay. He also knew the faster he worked, the faster he could get back to playing.

His phone vibrated again as he headed inside to grab the duffel bag he'd brought along. Isaac checked to find another message from Will.

Crazy, isn't it? The tide's finally turning, my friend.

The tide? Isaac stared at the screen, his gaze shifting from that line to the image of Katrina above it. *Oh no. Not yet.* He wasn't ready for this all to end.

"Do you have everything?"

"Yeah." He flashed her a forced smile and turned away, not wanting her to see the worry in his eyes. Because it was there again, big time. He snapped the lead on Louie's collar, grabbed his bag, and headed for the front door.

"Don't worry," he told Del over his shoulder. "We'll be back soon."

Chapter Sixteen

DEL HEADED TO her sister's for dinner Monday night, intending to help with more event planning while getting a partial kitchen pass for the evening. A side dish was requested, so she'd tossed a quick salad together. It was that or a bag of pretzels, her pantry running lower than normal thanks to a fun weekend that left little room for grocery shopping.

Not that she was complaining about all that Isaac-filled leisure time.

She'd texted him a few times throughout the day, and though he seemed to have helped avert yesterday's crisis, he sounded absolutely swamped again today. Not wanting to delay his progress, she'd tried leaving him alone as best she could. It wasn't how she'd hoped her Labor Day would go, but she completely understood. In business, deadlines happened. And if you wanted your business to stay afloat, you met those deadlines however you could.

"Where's little B?" she asked, joining Mia on the back porch. Her grill was fired up, burgers already sizzling on its grates.

"Rachel's house. They had a sleepover, been there all day. She texted a little bit ago and asked if she could stay for dinner. I figure between all her help at the bookstore and marching band practices, she deserved a fun day."

"She has been a busy girl lately. When's their first competition, anyway?"

"This coming weekend, so they'll be putting in extra hours the rest of the week."

"Wow, that came up quick. How are they sounding?"

"Not too bad." Mia grinned. "I always have to remind myself that they'll get better and better throughout the season."

Del helped herself to a glass of lemonade and took a seat at her sister's picnic table.

"That band stuff seems so hard. With sports, you just try getting better each season. With band, you guys toss out your old music and drill and start from scratch every year. Come on—that's brutal."

"Marching band is not for the faint of heart." Mia reached for her spatula and gave the burgers a flip. "Neither is dating. How are you two doing anyway, after his big announcement last week?"

"Announcement?"

"You know, that he's only here temporarily."

"Oh. Honestly, we haven't talked much more about it than what you heard. He believes they need him back east, so when it's time, he says he'll go."

"What do you believe?"

"That the company will do just fine without him. I mean, they've stayed afloat with him out here for nearly a year. How badly could they really need him there?"

Mia frowned. "Staying afloat and prospering are two different things, sweetheart. Besides, knowing Isaac, if there had been struggles along the way, he probably wouldn't have mentioned it to keep you from worrying."

"Says the queen worrier."

"I worry because I care," Mia said, throwing her a look over her shoulder. "And you do, too."

"Yeah, yeah." Heck, she was worried about him now, and he'd only been struggling with deadlines for one day. How would she react if this went on for days? Or weeks? "I just wish he would consider the alternatives, you know?"

"Have you asked him to?"

Had she?

Del tried to think back to their conversations surrounding the topic. But as much as he'd been open about the responsibilities waiting for him out east, she wasn't sure she'd actually admitted she wanted him to stay. Or asked him to consider continuing to work remotely.

"Surely he knows that's what I'm hoping for."

Mia turned to face her. "Sweetheart, he's a man. They need everything spelled out for them. Everything."

Delaney laughed. Yes, that'd been her experience over the years, too.

But she had to admit, Mia might be on to something. If Del asked him to stay, it would at least plant the seed in his mind. Hopefully, all the time they were spending together would help that seed grow. For tonight, though, she focused on girl time. With Isaac in the picture and all the event planning meetings, she and Mia hadn't gotten to just hang out much lately. And while she loved spending time with her new man, she had no intention of letting the rest of her relationships fall by the wayside. The chat with Isaac could wait.

Unfortunately, he sounded just as busy on Tuesday as he had on Monday. And on Wednesday. And Thursday. But after receiving big news at the talent show planning meeting that night, she decided to pop over to his place and surprise him with some warm cobbler. She rang the doorbell and waited, surprised there were no lights on inside. When Isaac answered the door, he joined her on the porch instead of stepping back to invite her in. The scruff on his chin was longer than usual, and there were bags under his eyes.

"Hey, Del. Everything okay?"

"Yep, just thought I'd bring my hardworking man a little dessert. Please tell me you're not too busy to remember to eat."

"Uh, no…"

He raked a hand through his hair, and Del knew he'd done precisely that.

"Wow, this must be one crazy big proposal."

"Multiple proposals, actually." He glanced back toward the front door. "I should keep working, but that cobbler does smell delicious."

Isaac dropped into a chair on his porch, and Del did the same. She dug into the bag and handed him a plastic container and fork, then took out one of each for herself. "I promise not to stay long. I was just missing you. And also, I had to share the big news!"

"Big news, huh?" he asked in between bites.

"Not sure if you know of them, but there's a huge, international musical instrument and equipment distributor down US 30, just before you get to Fort Wayne. They heard about our event and offered to loan us one of their portable stages and amazing sound systems…for free! That alone is saving us about a thousand dollars, but they also agreed to be a sponsor and donated another two thousand!"

"Wow, that's great, Del. You guys have got to be getting close to reaching your goal."

His words said one thing, his weary tone another. She studied his profile for a moment, this side of the porch shedding more light onto his ragged appearance. Clearly, the poor guy hadn't gotten much sleep this week.

"*Our* goal, buddy. You're a part of this, too. And you're right, we are getting really close. Aunt Faye is going to work up the numbers before our next meeting, but I have to think we're under five thousand to go. I had my doubts early on, but now I think between tickets and the food vendors, we may actually hit our goal."

"Or exceed it," he said, setting down his empty container. "I'm pulling for you all to do that. Then you'd have enough to restock the shelves that had water damage."

Again, with the "you all." What was with him tonight?

Isaac's knee began bouncing, his gaze roving from the porch to his front door. Whatever these deadlines were, they were weighing heavily on him. She put her cobbler back into the carryout bag and stood. She would not add to his stress levels.

"Did you get enough to eat?"

He nodded, not quite meeting her eyes.

"Then I'll let you go so you can get back to it. And here, hang on to this. You can reheat it later, when your stomach starts rumbling."

"That's very kind of you, but you take it," he said, rising to his feet. "I know how much you love cobbler."

"I'm full. Besides, I've got some ice cream at home that can tide me over until next time. You should take it."

He stared at the offered bag for a moment before accepting it.

"You're too good to me," he said quietly.

Del ducked to catch his downcast gaze. "That's what I'm here for. Try not to stay up too late working tonight, okay?"

She stepped closer and put her arms around him. Slowly, his encircled her as well. Del had missed this the past few days, missed his touch and warmth. She tipped her chin up to say as much, but was silenced by his lips crashing down on hers. Ecstasy flooded her as the kiss deepened, his hands curling into her hips. If he'd been sleepy before, the man was suddenly wide awake and kissing her breathless.

She heard the cobbler bag drop onto the porch's small side table, and suddenly Del was pinned to the siding, Isaac's hips pressed to hers. His mouth left hers to kiss a trail across her cheek and down her neck. He slid his hands under the hem of her shirt and tugged it up, granting him more skin to explore. Del sucked in a sharp breath as his fingers brushed across her bra, glad that they were hidden from the road by the woods around his house.

"Should we go inside?" she asked, surprised at how breathless she sounded.

Isaac didn't answer. Instead, he took her by the hand and led the way to his bed. Together, they worked out whatever pent-up frustration he was dealing with.

And it was *so* much better than the cobbler.

ISAAC LAY IN bed Saturday night, holding a sleeping Delaney in his arms, riddled with guilt. His time in Bourbon Falls was near its end—he could feel it. And rather than savor every moment with the woman he loved, he'd fallen back into his old habits, choosing to remain immersed in his work rather than out living life to its fullest.

Well, as full as it could be right now. But even that might soon be changing.

Will had kept a close watch on the TikToks that'd emerged the prior weekend, clips that clearly poked fun at Katrina's editing job. More videos had since surfaced, with thousands of people—mostly teens, interestingly enough—adding their own voiceovers to Isaac's rant. Most were cheesy, but a few were actually pretty funny. And since funny so often ruled the social media channel, the spinoffs had begun to go viral.

Which meant Katrina's credibility was slowly being flushed down the toilet.

Del snuggled closer. Could she hear his thoughts? Did she understand the implications? The dark cloud he'd prayed would leave him was beginning to dissolve, and with it, his time with her.

But he wasn't ready. He never would be.

He'd considered telling her about the videos tonight over dinner—carryout that she'd surprised him with once again—but he didn't have the heart to. Her smile had been too wide, her giving heart too big as usual.

As her smile had been yesterday when he'd looked outside to find Del and her niece in his yard, adding to the landscaping around the porch. She'd texted both him and Brooklyn earlier in the week, giving him the heads up that the girls were going to finish putting down rock and mulch. And though he hadn't been able to step away from his work, she'd still made it happen.

He didn't deserve her attention or her kindness, but somehow he'd earned both.

So rather than push her away tonight with doomsday warnings, he'd accepted her gifts and then made love to her, needing her to know—to feel—how much she meant to him when the words wouldn't come. And while she moved above him, eyes bright and beautiful smile full, he committed the view to memory, fearing it might well be their last time together.

She wasn't willing to leave, and the call to return was coming.

It was only a matter of time.

Chapter Seventeen

"ISAAC REALLY HAS done an outstanding job, getting these logos uploaded in a timely manner," Margaret said at their Thursday meeting. "Whatever you're paying him with, keep it up."

She and Del exchanged a knowing smirk, which left Faye shaking her head.

"Please, spare us the details," said her aunt. "We're down to just a little more than two weeks to go, and I'm excited to announce that we filled our roster an hour ago!"

"We got all thirty spots filled?" Barbara asked.

"We did. *And* we've gotten several emails from other entrants still wanting to get in, asking if we'll allow it. Apparently, the website capped the applications at thirty and won't let anyone else submit an entry. Which means we have a decision to make: should we extend the number to thirty-five?"

"It'd be great to have the extra money," Del said. "How close are we to meeting our goal of twenty-five thousand?"

"We're sitting at twenty-four and some change now," Faye said.

A round of applause broke out, followed by a chant of "Thirty-five, Thirty-five..."

"But will the audience sit through thirty-five performances?" Mia asked. "My students can hardly sit through a forty-minute lesson, and they're better behaved than most adults."

"Maybe that's a good thing," Nan said. "If they get tired of sitting, they'll be more likely to get up and grab something to eat or drink from our vendors."

"Brilliant," Margaret said, rubbing her hands together. "But can Isaac make the changes without losing any of the information we've already collected?"

"Dunno," Del said. "But I can certainly ask."

After another few days of him being increasingly silent—and bowing out of her father's cookout—another surprise visit might be needed. Though, when their planning meeting went long, she decided to wait another day before popping in to check on him again. It was late, and she hated to interrupt what sleep he might actually be getting.

Hopefully, he'd allow himself some time over the weekend to catch his breath. Heck, if they had another bedroom marathon session like they'd had last Saturday, they would both need another weekend to catch their breaths.

Friday after work, Del snagged a pizza from Bourbon Barrel Pizza, a pair of fresh cinnamon rolls from the Sweet Mash—sadly, they were out of cobbler—and a six-pack of Landshark from the GrabNGo, then turned her truck toward Elm Road. His garage door was up when she arrived, so she looked around the yard for him. Usually, the door only went up when he was cleaning up after Louie.

Not seeing him or his bully, Del gathered the pizza and rolls and headed for the front porch; she'd circle back for the beers after handing off the rest of their goodies. Struggling to see past the ginormous pizza box, she bumped the doorbell with her near elbow.

No answer.

On a frown, she rang the bell again. Four-legged trotting sounded on the other side of the door, followed by a familiar soft woof. She stepped back, ready to say, "Surprise!" but as the door swung inward, the word died in her throat. It was Isaac who stood in the doorway, she knew, but...it wasn't. Gone was his typical workout attire, replaced with pressed khaki shorts and a nice polo shirt. The view became even more unfamiliar as her gaze traveled northward to find his face completely clean shaven, its sexy scruff missing. But his hair was the most shocking—it'd been cut, the soft tendrils that used to curl at his collar now gone.

"Isaac...?"

"I'm sorry, but now isn't a good time, Delaney," he said, his gaze not quite meeting hers. "You should go."

A shadow passed across the light streaming in from the French doors that led to the back porch.

"But, I thought you might need—"

The French doors opened, and an unfamiliar male voice

rang out. "Was someone at the door?"

As Del watched, a man about Isaac's age stepped inside and made his way toward them. She didn't recognize him as anyone from around here, yet he moved through Isaac's place as though it was his own. He came to a stop just short of where they stood, Del's gaze following the movement. That's when she noticed the dining room behind him held more boxes than usual. And several partially packed suitcases.

Suddenly, the mental light bulb went on:

The stranger was Will McManus, and he was here to take Isaac home.

She looked to Isaac, shock rendering her mute. He had to have known Will was coming—he'd shaved and gotten a haircut, for crying out loud! Yet he hadn't bothered to pick up his cell phone and give her the heads-up.

Had he even planned to tell her he was leaving?

ISAAC STOOD IN his doorway, watching helplessly as Del's gears turned. If only he'd pressed the send button on his phone one of the hundred times he'd picked it up to call her this week instead of chickening out every time, they wouldn't be in this predicament right now. But he hadn't wanted to hurt her, hadn't known where to begin. Even now, he struggled to string a complete sentence together.

"Will," he said slowly. "This is Delaney. My—"

"Uber Eats driver." She raised the delivery boxes higher, a forced smile on her lips.

Isaac felt his jaw drop. Was she trying to bail him out, even now? He cringed. Maybe she hadn't quite connected all the dots. But surely, finally seeing him completely disguise-free should have been a clue. The haircut and shave had been Will's idea on their way back from the South Bend airport. Afterward, Isaac had hardly recognized the man staring back in the mirror.

"Oh. Great." Will patted his pockets. "Uh, just let me find my wallet."

"No need," Del said sweetly. "You can just put it on Isaac's tab."

"You've got an open tab?" He stepped around an immobile Isaac to take the offered boxes. "This pizza must really be something. You'd better call and get that settled up before we leave tomorrow."

Del's eyes widened for a brief moment, then narrowed to mere slits as Will walked away. Yep, the dots were now fully connected. This was definitely not how Isaac had hoped their good-byes would begin.

"Are you even kidding me right now?" she asked in a hiss.

"I was going to tell you. It just all happened so fast."

"And yet you had time to get a haircut and a shave."

Oh yes, the dots were now securely connected.

"It's too bad you didn't get any beer to go with this pizza," Will called from the kitchen. "Do you guys deliver that, too?"

"We do," she said through clenched teeth. "Just not to this house anymore."

Isaac looked toward her truck and spied the open side door. Maybe it was good she had planned to make two trips. Judging by the red in her cheeks, he might have ended up with a bottle cracked over his head.

"Del, I—"

"Save it for your call in to the *manager* later," she said in a low growl. "Unless, of course, you plan on dodging that conversation, too."

With that, she spun on her heel and stormed for the silver pickup parked in the drive. Dammit, this was not how he wanted to leave things between them. Hell, he didn't even want to leave. He wouldn't if his responsibilities weren't dictating that he did.

"Shoot," Will said from inside, his cell phone buzzing. "I've got to take this call."

He answered the phone and headed for the back porch with the box of pizza still in hand, giving Isaac the chance to chase after Del. He caught up with her just as she was reaching for her door handle.

"Del, wait."

She turned to face him, fury brewing in her eyes. "Why, so you can feed me some half-baked excuse for why you didn't bother to tell me you were leaving?"

"I was going to tell you. I pulled up your number to call more times that I can count. I just…couldn't bring myself to say good-bye."

"Then I'll do it for you. Good-bye, Isaac. Best of luck in New York City."

She turned again to go, but he caught her arm. "Del, *please*."

He half expected her to turn around swinging. Instead, thankfully, she paused. Didn't turn around, but she paused. Isaac released her and took a step back, glancing briefly toward the house to make sure the coast was still clear.

"I got a text from Will not long after Margaret's party. Apparently, someone made a bunch of TikToks that didn't paint Katrina and her extreme behavior very favorably. He was keeping an eye on them, with high hopes that they would help turn the tide."

"That's why you were so busy 'working'?" she asked with air quotes.

"No, we've really been racing to meet several deadlines. But the more Will texted, the more I could see the writing on the wall."

"And you didn't tell me."

Not a question but a quiet accusation. "I hoped I was wrong, but I shut down, started distancing myself from you. I hoped if I did that, it'd make it easier to part ways."

"Totally explains why you invited me in both times I stopped over." She threw a dark look over her shoulder.

"The first one was an accident. Well, I mean, *nothing* about what we did inside was an accident, but I hadn't meant for that to happen. And the second one, I just… I needed to be with you, to hold you one last time, in case my prediction was right."

"Would have been nice to be in on that little tidbit," she said. "I could have told you no and spared us from having this conversation."

A fair jab, but it still stung like hell.

"Would you have?" he asked softly. "Told me no?"

She didn't answer, but the tightness in her jaw called her bluff.

"After you left, I held out hope that I was wrong. Even prayed about it. When Will called Wednesday to tell me it was over, I disconnected and promptly threw up. Partially from relief, mostly because it meant my time with you was done."

"And that made you throw up?"

"Because I don't want it to be."

"Then stay." She turned to face him. "Don't go back with him. Take a stand against Will and start doing what *you* want to do."

"It's not that simple, Delaney." He pinched the bridge of his nose. If only there was an easy way to make her understand. "And Will isn't the bad guy here. He's my friend and my business partner. If it hadn't been for his idea to rent this place, I might have had to sell my half of the company and take up two-bit jobs working out of my apartment for the foreseeable future because nobody was gonna hire a guy the internet hated. We make our decisions together."

"But it's worked. You, living here and still working. Why do you keep insisting that you have go back?"

"But that's just it—it hasn't worked. Not well, anyway. With business picking back up these last few weeks, the programming team has floundered without me there to lead them. Will is excellent at what he does, but programming is not his forte. Our last video conference call was the ugliest we've ever had, the staff stressed and frustrated by the lack of leadership. I caused all of that, and now it's time I return and fix it."

She threw her arms out. "So go out east for a few days, fix it, and then come back to Bourbon Falls!"

"Delaney," he said softly. Tears filled her eyes. She turned away, his strong, confident woman refusing to look weak in front of him. "Please try to understand. I have to do this."

She stared at the ground for a long moment, and it damn near killed him not to pull her into his chest. But to do that might give her hope that he'd changed his mind. A hope he wasn't able to fulfill. Her shoulders rose and fell on a long, slow breath, then her chin rose high once more.

"Good luck with your company," she said. "I hope you get out east and are able to pick up right where you left off."

With that, she climbed into her truck and turned the

engine over. The driver's side window had been left down, and the bittersweet chorus of Kenny Chesney's "Knowing You" tumbled out.

"Good-bye, Isaac."

Her voice broke on his name, giving his heart a painful squeeze.

"Don't go yet. Just stay, so we can talk through this."

"Can't."

She shook her head, a single tear slipping down her cheek as the window rolled closed. Delaney Brooks turned her giant pickup around, drove down his driveway…

And out of his life.

Chapter Eighteen

DEL TOOK THE long way home from Isaac's that night, needing time to cry it out with her country music station. Because that's what she did when her heart was heavy—she drove and she cried. Best to get it out of her system when no one else was looking. Goodness knew, she didn't need Mia and the others worrying about her.

Damn Isaac and his unswerving sense of responsibility. But had she really thought he would choose differently?

The answer, of course, was no. They'd been having fun, a fling, nothing more—how many times had she insisted that was the case? Deep down, though, she'd started to believe they were growing into something more. That they *could* grow into something more. That maybe she even wanted them to grow into something more.

Unfortunately, it seemed fun was as far as it was ever going to get between them. Had they had more time, she might have been able to change his mind and convince him to stay. But those damned TikTapToe videos had surfaced and foiled her plans, making her hate technology that much more.

Sleep eluded her most of the night, her mind restless and bed feeling more empty than usual. Ridiculous, given that up until a few weeks ago, she'd been the only one to ever sleep in it. Maybe it was time to get a pet and help fill the bed. A cat, perhaps. Or maybe a dog.

An English bulldog.

Louie's face sprang to mind, triggering a fresh round of tears. Darn it, she was already missing him too. She grabbed her extra pillow and held it close, pretending it was him but without the snoring. Pretending Isaac was still there, and that this entire day had just been some terrible, awful dream.

The sound of a cell phone buzzing woke her some time later. She reached past a pile of discarded tissues to answer it, groggy and disoriented.

"Hello?"

"Del? Are you still in bed?"

Hearing the concern in Mia's voice, she glanced at her nightstand clock. Was it really ten thirty? Thank goodness today was Chase's Saturday to work. "Uh, no. I was just, um, in midthought. Working on a new landscape design."

She shifted into a seated position, trying not to feel guilty about the lies. But she wasn't ready to tell Mia what had happened. Not yet, anyway.

"Oh, that's great! I promise not to keep you long. Just checking to see if you and Isaac had any luck changing the number of allowed entries on the website last night."

Shoot, the entries change—she'd forgotten all about it.

Heck, after walking up to find him looking like a complete stranger, their website had quickly become the *last* thing on her mind.

"It didn't come up, actually."

"Too busy making out again, huh?" Mia laughed softly. "Well, see what you can find out today and let me know. Really, if he can't make the change, it's not the end of the world."

Del promised she'd try and disconnected, her gaze shifting to the muted sunlight filtering through her bedroom curtains. Was he even still in town to ask? Will had said "tomorrow," but she had no idea what time they were leaving. Could she even face him and keep it together, knowing he would soon be gone?

That's when the tiniest of hopes lit in her chest. She'd calmed down since their messy good-bye—maybe he had, too. Maybe he'd even taken to heart what she'd said and reconsidered.

Yes, it was a long shot—a really, really long shot—but she had to know.

In record time, she freshened up, dressed, grabbed a cup of coffee, and flew out the door. She kept the radio off on her drive out of town, emotions still too raw from a few popular songs she'd cried along with last night. Besides, the quiet would give her time to think of what she'd say when she got there.

Isaac, please don't go.

Isaac, I want you to stay.

Isaac, I—

Her breath hitched at the sight of a FOR RENT sign now posted in his yard. Del turned into his drive and slowly made her way up its winding path, unsure of what she would find on the other side of his woods. The view that awaited looked far different from the one she'd left last night: the garage door was shut, the porch empty of furniture and overhead light left on.

Don't panic. Maybe they're still inside packing.

An unseasonably cool breeze greeted her as she stepped from the truck. She swallowed hard and made for his front door, hoping, praying they were still here. No one answered her second round of knocking, and she chanced a peek in through the front window.

No boxes, no recliner. No Louie.

No Isaac.

She sank onto the edge of the porch as reality set in. He was gone. And she'd never shared how she really felt about him.

Del's stomach twisted, her skin suddenly clammy. She hurried around the side of the house and lost what little her stomach held.

Dammit, she hated throwing up.

Then again, it'd kept her from crying, so there was that. Emotionally drained, she made for her truck and the emergency bottle of Scope. Funny, hadn't Isaac thrown up after learning he was leaving too?

Too much puking, not enough talking.

And now it was too late.

She took one last look at the house, the yard that until yesterday had become a place she couldn't wait to visit, then climbed into her truck and headed west instead of back into town. She didn't need to go home and cry some more. She needed to think, to process everything that had transpired over the last few weeks. The best place to do that, of course, was on her tree swing.

The familiarity of gravel crunching beneath her tires brought her no joy today, nor did the sight of fluffy growing ducklings scurrying after their mama as her truck approached. Rex wasn't on the porch to help bring a smile to her face, likely still relegated to the indoors while her father monitored the seizures, and her dad wasn't out in the yard. Why did her whole world feel so dreary today?

Because Isaac had happened, that's why.

She settled onto her favorite childhood seat, leaned her elbows onto her knees, and closed her eyes. In an instant he was there, the memory so fresh that she could still imagine the way his cologne smelled. Could still hear his voice, feel his touch. She ached with a longing to have it all back again.

But she couldn't. He was gone.

"I've learned over the years that you sit differently on that swing depending on what's troubling you. When your mind is busy, you lean back. When your heart is heavy, you lean forward."

On a humorless laugh, Del turned to spy her father easing onto the lawn beside her. "Sometimes you're too smart for your own good, Pops."

"Your mother used to tell me the same thing." He winked. "So who's gone and broken my sweet pea's heart this time?"

She looked to the grass beneath her feet, its green beginning to fade with fall nearly upon them. "No one to blame but myself this time. Got a little too close to the flame. Should have known better."

"Should have known better than to get near the fire or one flame in particular?"

"One. Any of them. What difference does it make?"

"I take it Isaac left then."

She sat up and met her father's gaze. "How did you know?"

"Brooklyn. She was here earlier in the week, helping me feed the ducklings. Told me all about this Isaac and how some crazy ex-girlfriend of his had started a smear campaign online. She knew how much he meant to you, so she got a few of her friends together and they made their own videos, calling out this woman for the nutcase that she was in the hopes that it would clear Isaac's name. I thought she did a pretty nice job with them."

"*Brooklyn* made those videos?"

Del hung her head. Oh, the irony. The girl who'd

brought them together had ultimately driven them apart.

"She was trying to help."

"Oh, she helped, all right," Del said. "Helped me see what an idiot I was for starting to care about him."

"Sweet pea, there is nothing more beautiful in this world than caring for other people. The tricky part for some of us is that we start focusing too much on everyone else and forget to make sure our own wants and needs are met."

She snorted. "I don't *need* a man, Pops."

"But you wanted this one."

No. Maybe.

Oh, who was she kidding? "Yes."

A smile curled the corners of his lips. "Then do what you need to do to get him back."

"You make it sound so easy," she said, toeing the ground. "He left, went back to his other life. I'm still here."

"And?"

"What, you expect me to drop everything and chase after him? Pops, Bourbon Falls is what I love. There's nowhere I'd rather be than my hometown. If"—she swallowed hard—"the people I care about can't see that, then it's their loss, not mine."

"I think it's both your loss," he said with a sad smile. "With love comes compromise. In my experience, the couples whose relationships last are the ones who work together to decide what they're comfortable giving. And what they're open to receiving."

With that he rose, planted a gentle kiss on her head, and made for the duck pond. Pops always seemed to know when to offer his wisdom, and when to leave you alone to let it sink in. Today, though, his wisdom wasn't making sense.

Was he really telling her to leave all that she loved?

Del lifted her feet, sending the swing in motion. As it swayed, she processed.

Back. Isaac was gone.

Forth. She could go after him.

Back. She had a business to run.

Forth. So did he.

Back. He'd left.

Forth. He said he didn't want to…because of her.

Had she given up too quickly? Had her pride gotten in the way again, kept them from talking things out, exploring alternatives together?

It sure had. She'd gone storming off, even while he was asking her to stay and work things out.

Damn, she hated when Pops was right.

She'd sat around all these years after Jonathan, waiting for the perfect man to come walking into her life. Then, when an amazing one finally had, she'd given up on him the minute they ran into a complication instead of trying to work things out.

Instead of doing the adult thing: finding a compromise.

But how could they possibly work this out? They both had business responsibilities, and she had a town and bookstore to support. And a long-distance relationship was unappealing—she didn't want to have to wait weeks or months to see him next.

But she hated the thought of never seeing him again even more.

Maybe she should reach out to him, see if he was still open to having the conversation she'd refused to have last night. To give this crazy thing called compromise a try. No, not quite yet. First, she needed to fulfill her obligations with the fundraiser. If he could remain dedicated to his commitments, then of course he would understand her doing the same. And second, she needed to have some ideas lined up, in case he was willing to hear her out. Hopefully, she could come up with a few ideas by the time next weekend's fundraiser was over. Then she'd make the call.

In the meantime, Del would pray for those ideas to come—and that, when the time was right, Isaac would be open to listening.

ISAAC SAT IN his living room the following Sunday, staring at the television. Yes, his Giants were playing—and beating the Jets *soundly*—but neither the game nor his team's lead was bringing him joy. Heck, nothing had since his return to the Big Apple.

What did he expect, when he'd left the one person who

brought him so much joy back in Indiana?

Thank goodness for Louie. Without him, Isaac would have been utterly lost this past week. His bully was on the leather sofa beside him now, chin resting on Isaac's leg. The bulldog had been his shadow all week, struggling with separation anxiety each time his human left the apartment to go to work.

As if Isaac needed anything else to feel guilty about.

Thunder sounded in the distance, the vibration making Louie snuggle closer. A glance toward his balcony found swirling, dark clouds approaching.

Had Bourbon Falls had storms today, too? Would the bookstore's roof hold up until the talent show on Saturday? Would the event be enough of a success to pay for a new roof?

"Gotta let it go, man," he muttered to himself and took a long drag of his beer. He'd struggled with letting go all week, his mind still wrapped up in the recent past when it should have been focused on re-adapting to the crazed pace of NYC. But the Landshark label in his hand—not one of his usual Miller Lites—proved he'd been unsuccessful in keeping his thoughts away from Bourbon Falls and a certain landscaper he was missing something fierce.

Isaac leaned his head back on the top of his sofa, closed his eyes…and Del was there above him, naked and beautiful. He'd never met a woman like her before and doubted he ever would again. Funny and smart, confident and selfless. He'd enjoyed every minute of their time together, from her luring him out of his comfort zone to them making love in his bed. And damn, he missed it all.

It was cruel, really, that fate would drop him into an unfamiliar town, have him cross paths with the best thing that had ever happened to him, and then expect him to walk away a few short weeks later. That had to have been one of the hardest things he'd ever done—walking away. Especially after completely botching his good-bye.

He'd hoped to sneak off, leave town without having to face her. Without having to see the look of hurt or disappointment in her eyes. But just like Del, she'd come to check on him, being her usual, caring self. And just like him, he'd said all the wrong things and made their final good-bye that much worse.

The image of those monster cinnamon rolls from the Sweet Mash haunted him anew. Del had gone out of her way to surprise him after the hellacious week he'd had. A week he'd spent working and avoiding her rather than carving out time to enjoy their last few days together.

He didn't deserve her. He probably never had.

A stronger rumble from the oncoming storm shook the apartment. Louie climbed onto Isaac's lap and stretched across his chest. The weight was somewhere between slightly suffocating and comforting, and Isaac clung to him like a child would to a giant stuffed animal. He just wished it would make the ache in his chest go away.

Sure, he'd known leaving Delaney would be hard but never dreamed it'd affect him like this. He couldn't sleep, barely ate, and struggled to keep focused at work. Heck, he'd nearly missed his subway stops twice last week, lost in daydreams of what could have been.

And though a week had gone by, keeping her off his mind wasn't getting any easier. Hard to do when everywhere he looked, something reminded him of her: silver pickups, the beer in his fridge, advertisements for diners, ice cream stands, pizzerias. If he didn't do something to shut these memories off, he worried he'd lose his mind.

Even worse, he'd not heard a peep from her. In all fairness, being the chicken he was, he hadn't reached out to her, either. Plus, the fundraiser was less than a week away—he could only imagine how busy they all were with the preparations.

That lame excuse only made him feel worse; he should have been there, helping.

Maybe knowing that she was doing okay would help ease the pain. Surely, if she could find the strength to move on, so could he. Isaac grabbed his phone and scrolled to find her number, then stopped to think. A text out of the blue could be misinterpreted—he didn't want to give her false hope that he was coming back. If he'd learned anything this past week, it was that him being away had left a much bigger void in M&M's leadership team than he'd realized. As of yesterday, he'd managed to put out the biggest fires, but there were still several dozen more, smoldering and in need of his attention.

So, no, he didn't want to mislead her any more than he already had…which had him instead choosing the only other name and number he'd kept from Bourbon Falls: Brooklyn. It took him several tries before settling on a message that sounded harmless enough.

Hey, B. You guys all ready for the big event next weekend?

Yeah.

He sighed. Teens today. *Glad to hear, hope it's a huge success.*

She responded with "thanks." Definitely not giving him much to work with. Time to stop beating around the bush.

How's your aunt doing?

This time, her response took longer to arrive. *Are you asking because you feel bad or because you still care?*

Blunt as ever, but both fair questions.

Both.

Then why did you leave?

Ouch. And again, fair. *Because of work.* He thought for a moment, then added,

And because I'm an idiot.

That's what she said. An emoji followed, the winking smiley face with its tongue sticking out. *So what are you going to do about it?*

Isaac stared at Brooklyn's question. There it was, the fork in the road. He could either stay the course and be miserable for the foreseeable future or choose a different path in the pursuit of happiness. And man, being miserable sucked. But could he really step outside the rigid lines he'd lived within all these years and chase after what his heart wanted instead of what his mind said was right?

Wait—his heart?

Warmth that had nothing to do with Louie spread through his chest. All these years he'd been so focused on his career and getting their company off the ground that he'd never really given the notion of a serious relationship much thought. Now, it was all he could think about.

Delaney was all he could think about.

But could he really do this? Could he find a way to strike the perfect balance between work and play? Between work and…love?

To win back a certain blue-eyed beauty in Bourbon Falls, he was willing to give it a try.

I'm going to find a way to make it right.

It was time to fight for what he wanted—for *all* of what he wanted. But to make it work, he would need to think outside the box, to come up with an entirely new strategy. Something that wouldn't just help him find his way back to Del, but benefit his entire company, too.

He hadn't just spent the last year doing everything he could to save M&M only to walk away and abandon it now.

A plan began to form in his mind, one he hadn't considered before. One that could revive their business, correct some of their current pain points, allow for employee advancement, and position them for nationwide growth. He grabbed a notepad and pen, diagramming it out.

Yes, this could work. But would Will be on board with this big of a change?

Only one way to find out.

He dialed his best friend, invited him over for pizza, and hurried to prepare the sales pitch of his life.

Chapter Nineteen

DELANEY BREATHED A sigh of relief as the last act of the Bourbon Falls Talent Show got underway. It'd been a long and crazy day, hers starting many, many hours before the first spectators arrived, but it'd also been filled with much joy and laughter. All of their participants had done a phenomenal job preparing their acts and keeping them kid-friendly. To her knowledge, there'd only been one accidental f-bomb and that'd been from her sister Mia after stubbing her toe behind the sound system table.

Thankfully, that'd been before their spectators had arrived as well. Brooklyn, however, had been present and had spent the day teasing her mother about it.

"Even moms slip up now and again, you know," Mia had conceded shortly after intermission.

"Even amazing moms like yours." Del had given her sister a hug, then dug out a twenty and handed it to Brooklyn. "Now stop harassing her and go get me something tasty from the food trucks. I'm starving."

She checked the time on her phone. Goodness, two hours had passed since Brooklyn had brought her a grilled cheese sent straight from heaven. Judging by the lines forming around the food trucks and tents, their audience was getting hungry again.

"Eat, my pretties," she whispered. "Eat all you want. We've got a roof to pay for."

"What are you over here mumbling about?"

She turned to find Margaret, Barbara, and Nan approaching, each with a partially consumed adult beverage in hand. And, knowing them, not their first of the day, either.

"Just quietly encouraging people to keep buying food and drinks." She tipped her head toward their cups. "Thank you for your patronage."

"It's not like we had much of a choice, with as hot as it turned out to be today," Margaret said, fanning herself. "You'd think the talent show had fallen in the middle of July, not early October."

"It did turn out to be a hot one today," Del agreed. "Still better than thunder and lightning."

From the sound booth, Mia raised a red card in the air.

"Sorry, ladies, that's my cue. Time to thank our contestants and tell everyone to go and vote for their favorites."

Brooklyn's idea had been genius, creating a simple app to collect votes so the crowd could choose today's winners. A few dozen of her marching band buddies had even volunteered to help collect votes from people in the audience who didn't have app capabilities. Spectators would be helping choose winners in three age categories and then one act to accept their grand prize of two thousand dollars.

"Yep, you just get up on that stage and take care of business," Margaret said, shooing her.

"Oh, I will," Del said with a laugh. Heck, the hard part of the day was done for her. No more struggling with names as she introduced performers. Even with a serious case of early jitters, she was proud to not have even needed her secret stash of Scope today.

The Scope she hadn't needed since—

Nope, not gonna go there. Yes, she still missed Isaac terribly, and yes, she'd scanned the audience for him throughout the day, holding out hope that maybe he'd had a change of heart and would come back to see the show. But, of course, he wasn't here. After two weeks of her not texting, why should she expect anything different?

All that would change tomorrow, however. She'd put a lot of thought into what she would say to him, what compromise she might be able to offer. No, a long-distance relationship wasn't ideal, but she was willing to give it a try. Besides, her business slowed to almost nothing over the winter every year. Maybe she could start spending winters on the East Coast.

Unless, of course, he'd already written her off.

Would he take her call? Accept her offer? She didn't know. But until this fundraiser was complete, that answer was going to have to wait. She owed it to her hometown to stay focused on the task at hand.

Del waited for the final group—ten college coeds dressed in glittery chicken costumes—to vacate the stage, then made her ascent once more.

"Let's give another round of applause for the Dancing Cluckers, shall we?"

She turned off her microphone to clap along, her gaze scanning the crowd to take it in once more. Before her were people of all shapes, colors, and ages, their blankets and folding chairs making the grounds beside the historic train depot look like a giant patchwork quilt. Judging by the smiles and cheering, this event had been a rousing success for her hometown. Now, all she could hope was that it'd be enough to save their beloved bookstore as well.

As the cheering tapered off, she turned her microphone back on. "Okay, I know you're all probably eager to get home, but we're not quite finished with you yet. As we mentioned earlier, the outcome of today's event depends on your participation. This was created to be a community event, and we want the community to vote on their favorite acts from today."

A fresh round of applause erupted.

"So, audience, you have ten minutes to get your votes in. If you were unable to download our event app, no worries—you can place your votes by finding our helpers in the audience wearing the neon yellow Triton Marching Brigade T-shirts. And of course, if you're hungry or thirsty, our food and beverage vendors in the back are happy to serve you. In fact, let's give them another round of applause for all they've done today."

From the food tents, Max Williams blew the audience a kiss, then bowed. Del glanced over to Mia at the sound booth, who was fanning herself. She could only guess it wasn't from the heat.

"All right, everyone, let's get to voting. Your time starts now."

Del took a seat on the front edge of the stage and waved to her father, approaching with an unopened water bottle.

"You did great, sweet pea," he said, handing it to her. "I've heard nothing but compliments from everyone I've passed today."

"Thanks, Pops. Not gonna lie, I was a nervous wreck this morning. But once I got up on stage, I settled in and was able to have fun with it. Maybe I missed my calling?" she said with a shrug.

"Maybe we'll just have to make this an annual event, to help raise funds for all our local charities," Faye said, joining her father. "The town is eating this up."

"It sure is."

Del looked out over the sea of smiles, grateful for each and every one of them. The only thing that would have made today even better would be if—

She shook her head, refusing to let that thought damper the moment. With a flick, she turned her microphone back on. "Five more minutes."

Pops and Aunt Faye got pulled into a nearby conversation, leaving Del to check her text messages. Brooklyn had promised to text the results to Del's phone in the correct order, to avoid chances of technical difficulties. As she scrolled, she heard someone in the audience comment that they thought there weren't any more acts coming. Del looked up, meaning to confirm that, when she caught movement on stage from the corner of her eye. It was a chestnut and white bulldog, wiggle-waddling toward her, with a giant red bow tied around his neck.

No, not just any bulldog.

"Louie?" she whispered, turning to pat the space beside her.

He wiggle-waddled faster, covering her in happy, slobbery kisses once he reached her waiting open arms. But if Louie was here, that meant…

Del's gaze flew to the side of the stage from where Louie had appeared. No Isaac.

Louie squirmed closer, demanding her full attention as usual. That's when she noticed a scroll attached to the red ribbon around his neck. She carefully extracted and unrolled it.

Dear Delaney,

I'm sorry about my human. He's not the brightest guy in the world. But he loves you with his whole heart. So much so, he convinced his company to permanently relocate him to Bourbon Falls so he can be closer to you. I hope you'll take him back, because I miss the way you scratch behind my ears just right.

Love, Louie

P.S. M&M took up a collection for your bookstore. My human has a check for five hundred dollars to give you if you promise not to slug him in front of everyone when he comes out on stage.

Isaac was moving back? To be with her?

She stared at the note, not believing what she was seeing. This meant she wouldn't have to give up Bourbon Falls, give up her family and friends and hometown and house to be with the man she loved. Yes, loved! How could she not, when he'd come back for her at the best possible time?

Del's breath hitched as she looked up to find Isaac approaching from across the stage. He was really here! And looking handsome as ever in a dark V-neck tee and jean shorts. Gone were the dark sunglasses he'd always hidden behind, but the Yankees cap remained. And he had it on backward.

Had she ever seen a more perfect sight in all her life?

ISAAC SLOWED A few paces from Delaney, aware that all eyes were once again focused on the stage. But it was only her gaze he cared about right now. She covered her mouth, tears welling in her eyes. He silently prayed for the courage to pull this off.

"Did you read Louie's note?" he called.

Del nodded.

"And do you promise not to punch me?"

Soft laughter sounded from those sitting nearest the stage. Del nodded again, rising slowly to her feet. One tear tumbled down her cheek.

"Please tell me those are happy tears this time," he said softly. "I don't want to hurt you ever again."

Del studied him for a moment, then shifted her gaze to the floor.

Oh no. He'd waited too long. Despair pricked at his chest. "Delaney?"

She swiped a hand across her cheek and looked to him, wearing that devil-may-care grin he'd fallen for from the start. "Then get over here and kiss your woman already. She's waited far too long for this one."

In two long strides he had her in his arms, his lips locked with hers. Applause and cat calls sounded around them, but Isaac didn't care. Delaney hadn't sent him away, and that's all he dared to hope for.

"But I thought working remotely wasn't working?" She drew back to meet his gaze.

"It wasn't, not the way we were structured before. But I was miserable without you." Louie planted his rump on the stage and leaned into Del's legs. "Okay, we both were. I knew the minute I left it was the wrong thing to do. It just took me another week of moping for the solution to present itself."

"And?"

He shrugged. "It's not working remotely if we have a second office in the Midwest."

"Really?"

The magical glow was back, the one that had lit her features the day he visited her at the bookstore. The one he'd do anything to bring back, time and time again.

"Yes, really." He grinned. "Vivvy got a well-deserved promotion to my former programming lead position out east, which frees me up to explore new territory out here. I'll still be answering questions and providing support as always, and I promised to make short trips back to New York as needed, but Vivvy will be able to provide the day-to-day leadership our team was missing. Once we develop a presence in the Midwest, I'll add on local staff to help keep things rolling."

"You're really staying this time?"

"I really am." He took her hands in his. "I love you, Delaney Brooks. And I will never, ever leave you again."

Her smile widened. "I love you, too, Isaac Robert Manning. And you sure as hell better not."

On a laugh he pulled her into his chest. Oh, how he'd missed her confident, sassy ways. Booing suddenly sounded from the front right of the stage, and Isaac looked up to find Margaret, Barbara, and Nan giving them thumbs down.

"Hugs? Is that all you got, Manning?"

With a grin, he proceeded to dip Del backward. On a

shriek, she looked up at him and said, “Show off.”

“Oh, you ain’t seen nothing yet.”

And he proceeded to kiss her breathless, dangling over the front row. Hopefully, the town would be talking about that kiss for years to come.

Epilogue

DELANEY STUDIED HER reflection in the bathroom mirror, checking to make sure her wig was on straight. Usually, her Halloween costumes for the Brooks family haunted hayride were a little more random and a lot more adult. This year, however, Brooklyn had ordered them all to dress as their favorite Disney characters. When she couldn't track down an acceptable Ursula costume, she'd changed movie themes and gone with Belle. And since she was the one doing the shopping, her two new roommates had been bought costumes to fit the same movie theme.

Which was fine. Louie made a better Beast than Sebastian, anyway.

It'd been three weeks since the bookstore fundraiser, which, thank the stars, had been a huge success. The final fundraiser tally came in at $26,342.59—enough to replace both the roof and water-damaged books as well as repaint the store's interior. Thanks to their region's generosity and warmer-than-usual weather, the roof had been completed a week later, just as Isaac and Louie were getting settled in with Del.

It'd been her suggestion they move in, after Isaac admitted he hated staying at Will's place any longer than necessary. She knew he wasn't a fan of the rental's dark and gloomy interior, and she was no longer a fan of sleeping alone. And here, Louie had his own comfy little doggie bed on the floor beside Isaac so there'd be no more hogging her pillow. It was taking some adjustments, having roommates after living alone for so long, but so far, they hadn't encountered anything they couldn't work through with a little patience and compromise.

"Uh, Del? A little help here?"

She grinned at the mild panic in Isaac's voice. Apparently, not everyone was used to dressing up for costume parties. Del stepped out into their bedroom and eyed the fine specimen of man standing before her closet's full-length mirror.

"What's the matter, Gaston?"

"I can't get this belt to stay in place." His reflection met her gaze. "Also, I look ridiculous."

"I'm going to have to disagree. Those leather boots look quite good on you."

"And the tights?"

She sashayed closer, lifted his red tunic, and gave his butt a squeeze.

"Scrumptious," she said, her brows doing a little dance.

Isaac groaned. "I appreciate the compliment—if that's truly what it was—but I don't know how I feel about prancing around like this in front of your family."

"Would you rather I pull out the Mrs. Potts costume?" she asked innocently. "I thought for sure you'd rather be a huntsman, but if tea kettles are more your style…"

He raised his hands in defeat. "No, I'm good. Well, as good as I can be, given that I'm wearing tights."

Del laughed. "Stop, you look quite dashing. And if it makes you feel any better, Faye talked Pops into going as the genie from Aladdin. He'll be painted blue from head to toe. And I think he'll be in a much skimpier tunic than you."

"I'm not sure I want to see that."

"I know it's crazy, but this is our thing. My family, we do a lot of stuff together. And if you haven't noticed by now, we have a lot of fun in the process." She came to stand before him, batting her eyes as she took both his hands in hers. "Please be Gaston for me tonight."

He studied her for a moment, then looked to the ceiling with a heavy sigh. "Fine. For you, I'll wear the silly tights."

"And the wig?"

"There's a wig that goes with this getup, too?"

"Yep, your ponytail is nearly as long as mine." She grinned. "Here, I'll help you put it on."

She stepped around a snoring Louie—who looked adorable in his blue velvet smoking jacket—to dig through the pile of packages on their bed. After a bit of searching, Del found the dark-haired wig. She walked it over to Isaac, then motioned for him to sit on her hope chest to bring him to a more manageable height. The hairpiece was cheaply made, and likely as itchy as the one she had on, too, but it was needed to complete the look.

"It's a good thing I love you," he grumbled as she tugged it over his real hair.

"You know, if you hadn't cut your hair before moving back to New York, you wouldn't have needed a wig."

"I'll be honest, I kinda miss having my hair longer. Which way do you like it best?"

Del leaned closer to straighten his wig and whispered in his ear, "Long enough for me to run my fingers through it."

He pulled her into his lap and nuzzled the soft spot beneath her ear. "Hmm. So how long is this hayride thing supposed to last?"

"Not too long, Brooklyn's got school tomorrow." She kissed him, then slipped out of his grasp to finish primping. If they started making out now, they'd never make the party—and everyone there would know why. "We'll do the hayride, then a bonfire with smores and hot apple cider. Mia should be bringing her semi-famous apple crisp, too."

"Apple crisp? Is it as good as Gina's cobbler?"

Del laughed as she set the last of his bobby pins in place. Thank goodness she'd fallen for someone with a sweet tooth as bad as hers.

"Depends who you ask. Personally? I think it's better."

"Better than Sweet Mash cobbler? Then what are we waiting for, woman? It's time to take this show on the road."

Isaac roused Louie and made the motion for *car ride*. The bully started his happy wiggle dance, then trotted after his hungry human into the front hall. Delaney grabbed the basket of books that went with her costume and followed them out, counting her blessings that everything had worked out for both the bookstore—and her heart—in the end.

The End

Want more? Don't miss the next book in the Bourbon Falls series, *Once Upon a Christmas Beauty*!

Join Tule Publishing's newsletter for more great reads and weekly deals!

Acknowledgments

Cliché as it may sound, this story—heck, this entire *series*—would not have come to be without the encouragement (and patience) of my amazing editor Julie Sturgeon. Thank you for "getting" all my Hoosier-isms and sharing yours with me.

To Tina, I thank you as always my dear friend, for the author talk and brainstorming sessions we shared during our walks, coffee chats, and marching band contest trips as this book was taking shape.

To Danielle and Jeremy, thank you for being my ever-encouraging beta readers—I rely on your feedback and positivity more than you know.

Many thanks as always to my sons for their understanding and support as my writing journey continues. Our many weekend soccer trips across Indiana helped me pick the perfect location for this series.

Thank you also to the wonderful team at Tule who worked tirelessly to make this book shine.

Lastly, my sincere gratitude to you, my readers. Thank you for spending your valued and finite time with me and the characters in Bourbon Falls.

If you enjoyed *Once Upon a Beast,*
you'll love the next books in the…

Bourbon Falls series

Book 1: *Once Upon a Beast*

Book 2: *Once Upon a Christmas Beauty*
Coming in October 2023

Book 3: *Once Upon a Summer Night*

Available now at your favorite online retailer!

More Books by Kyra Jacobs

Love at the Beach Shop
The Paradise Key series

Available now at your favorite online retailer!

About the Author

Kyra Jacobs is an extroverted introvert who writes of love, humor, and mystery in the Midwest and beyond. Her romance novels range from sweet contemporary to romantic suspense and paranormal/fantasy. No matter the setting, Kyra employs both comedy and chaos to help her characters find inspiration and/or redemption on their way to happily ever after.

When this Hoosier native isn't pounding out scenes for her next book, she's likely outside, elbow-deep in snapdragons or spending quality time with her sports-loving family. Kyra also loves to read, tries to golf, and is an avid college football fan.

Thank you for reading

Once Upon a Beast

If you enjoyed this book, you can find more from all our great authors at TulePublishing.com, or from your favorite online retailer.

TULE
PUBLISHING

Printed in the USA
CPSIA information can be obtained
at www.ICGtesting.com
LVHW041148081023
760500LV00030B/666

9 781959 988700